...S VERNE (1828–1905) was bc
...er 60 novels, and is famous for
..ravel. He is the author of such well
Centre of the Earth, Around the W. ...y *Days* and *Twenty*
Thousand Leagues under the Sea. In 1859 Verne travelled to
Scotland, a journey that inspired *The Underground City*, a new
translation of which was published by Luath Press in 2005.
Originally published as *Les Indes noires*, *The Underground City* is set
underneath Loch Katrine and was described by Michel Tournier as 'one
of the strangest and most beautiful novels of the nineteenth century'.
In 1879 Verne returned to Scotland, visiting Glasgow and travelling
to Oban, from where he went on a day cruise round Mull, Iona and
Staffa. His diary relates the details of his journey, which clearly
inspired the route that the travellers in *The Green Ray* follow, and
notes his interest in both Fingal's Cave and the Corryvreckan
whirlpool, which feature strongly in this novel, of all his books the
one that most closely follows Verne's travels in Scotland.

Inside illustrations are the drawings by L. Benett from the first octavo
edition of *Le Rayon vert* by Jules Verne, Paris 1882. Reproduced
courtesy of Professor Ian Thompson.

JULES VERNE

LE RAYON-VERT

DESSINS PAR L. BENETT

The Green Ray

A new translation of the complete text with illustrations

JULES VERNE

translated by Karen Loukes
with an afterword by Professor Ian Thompson

Luath Press Limited

EDINBURGH

www.luath.co.uk

First published as *Le Rayon vert*, Paris 1882
First published in English, London 1883
This translation first published 2009

ISBN: 978-1-905222-1-24

The paper used in this book is recyclable. It is made
from low chlorine pulps produced in a low energy,
low emission manner from renewable forests.

Printed and bound by
The Charlesworth Group, Wakefield

Typeset in 10 point Sabon
by 3btype.com

© Luath Press Ltd 2009

Brother Sam and Brother Sib

'BET!'
'BETH!'
'Bess!'
'Betsy!'
'Betty!'

One after another the names echoed through the magnificent Helensburgh hall. Brother Sam and brother Sib had the odd habit of summoning their housekeeper in this way. But at that moment those familiar diminutives of Elizabeth were no more capable of bringing forth that excellent lady than if her masters had called her by her full name. Instead the steward, Partridge, appeared at the hall door, bonnet in hand.

Partridge, addressing the two honest-looking gentlemen, who were sitting in the embrasure of a diamond-paned window whose three sides jutted out on the front of the house, said:

'You were calling for dame Bess, sirs, but she's not here.'

'Where is she then, Partridge?'

'She's with Miss Campbell, who is walking in the park.'

And, at a sign from the two gentlemen, Partridge retired gravely.

The gentlemen were the brothers Sam and Sib – christened Samuel and Sebastian – Miss Campbell's uncles. Scotsmen of the old school, Scotsmen of an ancient Highland clan, they had a combined age of one hundred and twelve with only fifteen months separating the elder brother, Sam, from the younger, Sib.

To give a quick sketch of these prototypes of honour, goodness and devotion, it is sufficient to state that their entire existence had

The communal snuffbox was opened by brother Sam...

been devoted to their niece. They were her mother's brothers. Her mother had been left a widow after one year of marriage, only to be carried off herself shortly afterwards by a lightening-quick illness. Sam and Sib Melville thus remained the small orphan's only guardians in this world. They were united in the same devotion; they lived, thought and dreamt for her alone.

For her sake they had remained single, and, moreover, they had done so without regret. They were of that number of estimable persons who have only one role to play down here, namely that of a guardian. And once again, is it not sufficient to say that the eldest had made himself the father of the child, and the youngest the mother? So, it sometimes happened that Miss Campbell greeted them quite naturally with 'good morning, papa Sam! How are you, mama Sib?'

To whom could they be better compared, these two uncles, though without the aptitude for business, than to those charitable merchants, so good, so united and so affectionate, the Cheeryble brothers of the city of London, the most perfect characters ever to have emanated from Dickens' imagination! It would be impossible to find a more accurate likeness, and, should the author be accused of having borrowed their type from that masterpiece *Nicholas Nickleby*, no one can regret this appropriation.

Sam and Sib Melville, linked by the marriage of their sister to a collateral branch of the ancient Campbell family, had never been parted. An identical education had made them mentally similar. They had had the same teaching at the same college in the same class. As they generally voiced the same ideas about all things using identical terms, either one could always finish the other's sentence using the same expressions emphasised by the same gestures. In short, these two individuals were as one. There was however some difference in their physical make-up. Sam was a little taller than Sib, Sib a little fatter than Sam, but they could have exchanged their grey hair without altering the character of their honest faces on which all the nobleness of the descendants of the Melville clan was imprinted.

Is it necessary to add that they shared a similar taste in the cut of their simple, old-fashioned clothing and in their choice of good Scottish fabric, although, and who could explain this slight difference, Sam seemed to prefer dark blue and Sib dark brown.

To be honest, who would not have wanted to live in the intimacy enjoyed by these two worthy gentlemen? Used to walking at the same pace in life, they would doubtless stop only a little way apart when the time came for their final rest. In any case, these two remaining pillars of the Melville house were solid. They might well support the ancient edifice of their race, which dated back to the fourteenth century, the epic era of Robert Bruce and of Wallace and the historic period in which Scotland disputed its right to independence with England, for a long time yet.

But though Sam and Sib Melville no longer had the chance to fight for the good of their country, though their lives were less fraught and had been spent in the peace and affluence that fortune bestows, they should not be reproached, nor should it be thought that their race had degenerated. They had, through their good deeds, continued the generous traditions of their ancestors.

Consequently, as they were both in good health and had not a single irregularity with which to reproach themselves, they were destined to age without ever becoming old, neither in body nor in mind.

Perhaps they had one fault – who can claim to be perfect? They peppered their conversation with images and quotations borrowed from the famous owner of Abbotsford, and more particularly from the epic poems of Ossian, which they doted upon. But who could reproach them for this in the land of Fingal and Walter Scott?

To finish the portrait with a final flourish, it should be noted that they were great snuff-takers. Now, everyone knows that in the United Kingdom a tobacconist's sign usually depicts a valiant Scot with a snuffbox in his hand, strutting about in traditional dress. Well, the Melville brothers might have appeared quite advantageously on one of these painted zinc signs which creak from the roofs of tobacconists' shops. They took as much snuff as, if not more snuff than, anyone on either side of the Tweed. But, characteristically, they only had one snuffbox between them – though it was enormous. This portable object passed in turn from the pocket of one into the pocket of the other. It was like an extra link between them. It need hardly be said that they always experienced the need to inhale the excellent narcotic powder, which they had brought in from France, at the same moment, were it ten times an hour. Whenever one of them drew the box out from the depths of his clothing, it was only to find that they both felt like a good pinch, and, whenever one of them sneezed, the other would say, 'God bless you!'

All in all, the brothers Sam and Sib were veritable children as far as the realities of life were concerned. They knew little enough about the practical things in the world, but about industry, finance and business they knew nothing at all, nor did they claim to. As far as politics went, they were, perhaps, Jacobites at heart, and retained some of the old prejudice against the reigning Hanover dynasty, thinking of the last of the Stuarts as a Frenchman might think of the last of the Valois. Finally, in affairs of the heart, they knew less again.

And yet the Melville brothers had only one thought on their minds. They wanted to see clearly into Miss Campbell's heart, and to divine her most secret thoughts. They wanted to direct them if necessary and develop them if need be, and finally they wanted to marry her to a good fellow of their choice, who could not fail to make her happy.

If they are to be believed – or rather to hear them speaking – it would seem that they had found precisely that good fellow who would bear the responsibility for that pleasant task here on earth.

'So, Helena has gone out, brother Sib?'

'Yes, brother Sam, but, as it is now five o'clock, it cannot be much longer before she returns home.'

'And when she returns...'

'I think, brother Sam, that it will be appropriate to have a very serious meeting with her.'

'In a few weeks, brother Sib, our girl will reach the age of eighteen.'

'The age of Diana Vernon, brother Sam. Is she not as charming as the delightful heroine of *Rob Roy*?'

'Yes, brother Sib, and in the grace of her manners...'

'The turn of her mind...'

'The originality of her ideas...'

'She is more like Diana Vernon than Flora MacIvor, the great and imposing figure in *Waverley*!'

The Melville brothers, proud of their national writer, cited several more names of heroines from *The Antiquary*, *Guy Mannering*, *The Abbot*, *The Monastery*, *The Fair Maid of Perth*, *Kenilworth* etc but all, according to their notions, were inferior to Miss Campbell.

'She is like a young rose tree that has grown a little fast, brother Sib, and which must...'

'Be given a stake, brother Sam. Now I was told that the best stake...'

'Must evidently be a husband, brother Sib, for he takes root in turn in the same soil...'

'And grows quite naturally, brother Sam, alongside the young rose tree that he protects.'

Together, the Melville brothers had found this metaphor; it was borrowed from the book *The Perfect Gardener*. Doubtless they were satisfied with it, as it brought the same smile of contentment to their good faces. The communal snuffbox was opened by brother Sam, who plunged two fingers into it delicately. It then passed into the hands of brother Sib, who, after having drawn a large quantity, put it into his pocket.

'So, are we agreed, brother Sam?'

'As always, brother Sib!'

'Even on the choice of stake?'

'Would it be possible to find a nicer one, or one more to Helena's taste, than this young scholar, who, on several occasions, has displayed such decent feelings...?'

'And so serious towards her?'

'Indeed it would be difficult. Educated, a graduate of the universities of Oxford and Edinburgh...'

'A physicist like Tyndall...'

'A chemist like Faraday...'

'Who knows the reason for everything in this world thoroughly, brother Sam...'

'And who would have an answer to any question, brother Sib...'

'The descendent of an excellent Fifeshire family, and, moreover, the possessor of an ample fortune.'

'Not to mention his, as it seems to me, highly pleasing appearance, even with his aluminium spectacles!'

Had the spectacles of this hero been made of steel, nickel or even gold, the Melville brothers would not have viewed them as a damnable vice. It is true that these optical devices suit young scholars well for they complement a slightly serious physiognomy perfectly.

But this graduate of the aforementioned universities, this physicist, this chemist, would he suit Miss Campbell? If Miss Campbell resembled Diana Vernon, who, as we know, felt nothing more for her scholar cousin Rashleigh than a restrained friendship, and who did not marry him at the end of the volume?

Never mind! That did not worry the two brothers. They brought to the affair all the inexperience of two old bachelors, who were quite incompetent in such matters.

'They have often met one another already, brother Sib, and our young friend does not appear insensible to Helena's beauty!'

'I think not brother Sam! Had the divine Ossian had her virtues, her beauty and her grace to extol, he would have called her Moina, that is to say beloved of the entire world...'

'Unless he had named her Fiona, brother Sib, that is to say the unrivalled beauty of the Gaelic era!'

'Did he not foretell of our Helena, brother Sam, when he said:

She left the hall of her secret sigh! She came in all her
beauty, like the moon from the cloud of the east...

'Loveliness was around her as light,' brother Sib. 'Her steps were the music of songs.'

Happily the two brothers ended their quotations at that

A young girl appeared, her cheeks glowing pink.

point, and fell back down from the somewhat cloudy regions of the bards into the realm of reality.

'Surely,' said one of them, 'if Helena is agreeable to our young scholar, he can hardly fail to please…'

'And if, on her part, brother Sam, she has not yet paid all the attention that is due to the great qualities that nature has so liberally bestowed on him…'

'It is only, brother Sib, because we have not yet told her that it is time for her to start thinking about marriage.'

'But once we have directed her thoughts that way, even assuming that she is somewhat prejudiced, if not against the husband, at least against marriage…'

'She will not be long in saying yes, brother Sib…'

'Like that excellent Benedick, brother Sam, who, after resisting for so long…'

'Marries Beatrice at the end of *Much Ado About Nothing*!'

Such was the idea of Miss Campbell's two uncles, and the conclusion of this scheme seemed as natural to them as that of Shakespeare's comedy.

They had risen of one accord. They smiled at each other knowingly. They rubbed their hands together in time. This marriage was decided! What difficulty could arise? The young man had asked for their consent. The young girl would give them her answer, which they had no need to worry about. All of the proprieties were satisfied. All that remained was to fix the date.

Indeed it would be a beautiful ceremony. It would take place in Glasgow but not at the cathedral of St Mungo, the only church in Scotland, alongside that of St Magnus on Orkney, that had been respected at the time of the Reformation. No! It is too vast and consequently too sad for a wedding. A wedding, according to the Melville brothers, should be a time when youth blossomed and love shone forth. Instead they would choose St Andrew's or St Enoch's, or even St George's, which belonged to the most fashionable district in town.

Brother Sam and brother Sib continued to elaborate on their projects in a manner that resembled a monologue rather than a dialogue, as they always expressed the same train of thoughts in the same way. As they talked, they looked out through the diamond panes of the vast window at the beautiful trees in the park, the trees that Miss Campbell was walking under at that moment, at the streams of running water framed by verdant flower beds, at the sky which was suffused with a radiant mist that seems peculiar to the Highlands of central Scotland. They did not look at one another, it would have been useless, but from time to time, through some kind of affectionate instinct, they took one another's arm or clasped one another's hand as if to better establish communication of thought through some sort of magnetic current.

Yes! It would be superb! Everything would be done grandly and nobly. The poor of West George Street, if there were any – and where were there not? – would not be forgotten in the celebration. In the unlikely event that Miss Campbell wanted the wedding to be a simpler affair, and if she insisted on making her uncles see reason, they would be firm with her for the first time in their lives. They would not give in on this point, or on any other. It would be with great ceremony that the guests at the wedding feast would drink to their heart's content. And brother Sam half extended his right arm at the same time as did brother Sib, as though they were exchanging the famous Scottish toast in advance.

At that moment the hall door opened. A young girl appeared, her cheeks glowing pink from the animation of a rapid walk. In her hand she waved an opened newspaper. She went up to the Melville brothers and gave them each two kisses.

'Good afternoon, uncle Sam', she said.

'Good afternoon, my dear.'

'How are you, uncle Sib?'

'Wonderful!'

'Helena', said brother Sam, 'we have a small arrangement to make with you.'

'An arrangement? What arrangement? What have you been plotting, dear uncles?' Miss Campbell demanded, looking from one to the other somewhat mischievously.

'You know the young gentleman, Mr Aristobulus Ursiclos?'

'Yes, I know him.'

'Do you dislike him?'

'Why should I dislike him, uncle Sam?'

'Then you like him?'

'Why should I like him, uncle Sib?'

'In short my brother and I, after some mature reflection, are thinking about proposing him to you as a husband.'

'Me! Marry!' cried Miss Campbell, letting off the merriest peal of laughter ever to be repeated by the echoes in the hall.

'Don't you want to marry?' said brother Sam.

'Why should I?'

'Ever?' said brother Sib.

'Never', replied Miss Campbell, putting on a serious air which was belied by her smiling mouth, 'never dear uncles, or at least not until I have seen...'

'What?' cried brother Sam and brother Sib.

'Not until I have seen the Green Ray.'

2

Helena Campbell

THE HOUSE IN which the Melville brothers and Miss Campbell lived was situated three miles from the small village of Helensburgh on the banks of Gare Loch, one of those picturesque lochs that capriciously indent the right-hand bank of the Clyde.

During the winter season, the Melville brothers and their niece occupied an old town house in West George Street in Glasgow in the aristocratic district of the new town, not far from Blythswood Square. They resided there for six months of the year, unless some whim of Helena's – to which they submitted without comment – took them off on some long trip in the direction of Italy, Spain or France. In the course of their travels, they continued to see only through the eyes of the young girl, going where it pleased her to go, stopping where it suited her to stop, admiring only what she admired. Then, when Miss Campbell had closed the album in which she recorded, either with pencil or with pen and ink, her impressions of the trip, they made their way docilely back to the United Kingdom, and returned to their comfortable abode in West George Street, not without some satisfaction.

When the month of May was around three weeks old, brother Sam and brother Sib would experience an immoderate desire to leave for the country. At exactly the same moment, Miss Campbell herself would display the not less immoderate desire of leaving behind Glasgow and the noise of a big industrial city, of fleeing the bustle of business that sometimes ebbed as far as the Blythswood Square district, and of once again seeing a sky that was less filled with smoke and of breathing air that was less saturated with

Miss Campbell, followed by the faithful Partridge…

carbonic acid than the sky and air of the ancient metropolis, whose commercial importance was established by the tobacco lords several centuries ago.

The entire household of masters and servants thus left for Helensburgh, which lay at a distance of twenty miles at the most.

It is a pretty place, the village of Helensburgh. It had been turned into a seaside resort, and was heavily frequented by all those who were at leisure to vary trips on the Clyde with excursions to Loch Katrine and Loch Lomond, both of which were popular with tourists.

The Melville brothers had chosen the best place for their country house, one mile from the village on the shore of Gare Loch, in a jumble of magnificent trees and in the midst of a network of streams, on undulating ground whose relief lent itself well to all that takes place in a private park. Cool shady areas, green lawns, clumps of trees and flower beds, fields whose 'healthy grass' was grown specially for a few lucky sheep, ponds whose water was a clear black and which were inhabited by wild swans, those graceful birds of which Wordsworth said:

The swan on still St Mary's Lake
Float double, swan and shadow!

In short, the summer residence of the wealthy family was composed of everything that nature can bring together to delight the eye without the hand of man playing a part in its arrangement.

It should be added that there is a charming view from the part of the park situated above Gare Loch. Beyond the narrow gulf on the right, the eye rests first of all on the Rosneath peninsula, on which stands a pretty Italian villa belonging to the Duke of Argyll. To the left the small village of Helensburgh stretches along the coast, its undulating line of houses interspersed with two or three imposing spires. Its elegant pier extends out over the waters of the loch for the service of steamers, and the hills in the background are enlivened by several picturesque dwellings. Opposite, on the left-hand bank of the Clyde, Port Glasgow, the ruins of

Newark Castle and Greenock with its forest of masts and plumes of multicoloured flags, form an extremely varied and captivating panorama.

And the view was even more beautiful from the top of the house's main tower from where it was possible to see yet more.

This square tower was ornamented with battlements and machicolations, and its parapet decorated with stone lace-work. Pepperbox turrets were suspended airily from three corners of its summit, whilst the octagonal turret on its fourth corner rose still higher. Here stood the inevitable flagpole which rises up on the roofs of all the houses and the sterns of all the ships in the United Kingdom. This sort of keep was of modern construction, and dominated the body of buildings that made up the house itself, with its irregular roofs, its capricious windows, its multiple gables, its projections standing out from the façade, its screens clinging to its windows and its chimneys with their finely carved tops – often graceful and yet extravagant items with which Anglo-Saxon architecture is enriched at will.

Now it is on this highest of the tower's platforms, beneath the national colours which flapped in the breeze off the Firth of Clyde, that Miss Campbell liked to dream for hours on end. She had turned it into a pretty refuge and an airy observation post, where she could read, write and sleep in all weather, sheltered from the wind, the sun and the rain. It is there that she was most often to be found. If she was not there, it was that a whim had led her to wander in the park, sometimes alone, sometimes accompanied by dame Bess, or that her horse had borne her off though the surrounding countryside, followed by the faithful Partridge, who had to hurry his own horse on so as not to lag behind his young mistress.

From amongst the numerous servants, special mention should be made of these two honest individuals, who had been attached to the Campbell family since their childhood.

Elizabeth, the 'lucky', the 'mother', as housekeepers are called in the Highlands, then numbered as many years as she had keys in her bunch, and there were no less than forty-seven of the latter. She was a real housewife; serious, methodical and knowledgeable, and ran the entire house. Perhaps she thought that she had brought up the Melville brothers, although they were older than she was, but what is certain is that she had bestowed maternal care on Miss Campbell.

Alongside this valuable stewardess stood Partridge, a servant who was absolutely devoted to his masters, and a Scot who remained faithful to the ancient customs of his clan. Invariably dressed in traditional Highland dress, he wore a colourful blue bonnet, a tartan kilt that came down to his knees, a sporran – a sort of purse made of long hair – long socks held up by garters and leather brogues.

With a dame Bess to run the house and a Partridge to look after it, what more is necessary for anyone wishing to be assured of domestic tranquillity here on earth?

It has doubtless been noticed that Partridge, when he came in response to the Melville brothers' call, referred to the young girl as Miss Campbell. Had the gallant Scot called her Miss Helen, which is to say by her Christian name, he would have committed an infraction of the rules that govern degrees of hierarchy – an infraction that is more specifically referred to by the word 'snobbery'.

In effect, the eldest, or indeed only, daughter of a member of the gentry is never known by the name by which she is christened, not even in the cradle. If Miss Campbell had been the daughter of a peer, she would have been called Lady Helena. Now the branch of the Campbells to which she belonged was only collateral, and was but distantly connected with the direct branch of the paladin Sir Colin Campbell, whose origin goes back to the Crusades. For many centuries, the branches emanating from the main trunk had grown further away from the line of their glorious ancestor to whom the Argyll, Breadalbane and Lochnell clans, amongst others, are connected. But however distant the relation was, Helena, through her father, had flowing in her veins a little of the blood of this illustrious family.

Still, though she was only Miss Campbell, she was none the less a true Scotswoman, one of those noble daughters of Thule with blue eyes and blond hair, whose portrait, engraved by Finden or Edwards and placed in the midst of the Minnas, Brendas, Amy

Robsarts, Flora MacIvors, Diana Vernons, Miss Wardours, Catherine Glovers and Mary Avenels, would not have detracted from one of those 'Keepsakes' in which the Scots like to bring together their great novelist's most beautiful feminine figures.

To tell the truth, Miss Campbell was charming. She was admired for her pretty face with its blue eyes – the blue of the Scottish lochs, as people say – her elegant figure, her somewhat haughty demeanour and her countenance, which was usually dreamy except when a hint of irony animated her features. In short, her whole person was stamped with grace and distinction.

And not only was Miss Campbell beautiful, she was good too. Though wealthy through her uncles, she did not seek to appear rich. She was charitable and applied herself to verifying the ancient Gaelic proverb: 'The hand that gives is the hand that gets'.

Above all, loyal to her region, clan and family, she was a Scotswoman in both heart and soul. She would have placed even the lowliest Sawney before the most important John Bull. Her patriotic soul vibrated like the strings of a harp when the voice of a Highlander singing some local pibroch reached her across the countryside.

De Maistre said, 'Within us there are two beings: myself and another.'

Miss Campbell's 'self' was serious and thoughtful, and saw life more from the point of view of her duties than of her rights.

Her 'other' was romantic, a little inclined to superstition, and loved the wonderful tales that arise so naturally in the land of Fingal. Like the Lindamiras, those delightful heroines who feature in tales of chivalry, she ran through the surrounding glens listening to the 'bagpipes of Strathearne', as the Highlanders call the wind when it blows along lonely paths.

Brother Sam and brother Sib loved both sides of Miss Campbell equally. It should however be confessed that, if the former charmed them with her reason, the latter possessed the capacity to disconcert them sometimes with her unexpected rejoinders, her capricious flights up to the heavens, and her sudden gallops into a land of dreams.

And was it not this 'other' who responded so oddly to the proposition that the brothers had made?

'Marry?' the 'self' would have said, 'Marry Mr Ursiclos...! We will see... we will talk about it!'

'Never! Or at least not until I have seen the Green Ray!' the 'other' had responded.

The Melville brothers looked at each other blankly, whilst Miss Campbell settled down in the large Gothic armchair in the recess of the window.

'What does she mean by the Green Ray?' asked brother Sam.

'And why does she want to see this ray?' replied brother Sib.

Why? We are going to find out.

3

The Article in the
Morning Post

ANYONE INTERESTED IN physical curiosities might have read the following in that day's *Morning Post*:

> Have you ever watched the sun as it sets over the sea? No doubt the answer is yes! Have you followed it up to the moment when the upper part of its disc grazes the line of the water and it is about to disappear? Very probably. But have you ever noticed the phenomenon that is produced at the exact moment when the radiant star sends forth its last ray, if the sky is free from haze and perfectly pure? Perhaps not. Well, when you first have the opportunity of making this observation, and it is one that offers itself very rarely, it will not be a red ray that strikes the retina of your eye, as might be expected; it will be a 'green' ray. It will be a ray of a wonderful green hue, a green that no painter is able to obtain on his palette, a green the like of which nature has never produced, not in the many varied shades of plants, or in the colour of the clearest seas! If the colour green exists in Paradise, it can only be of this shade, which is, without doubt, the true green of Hope!

Such was the article in the *Morning Post*, the newspaper that Miss Campbell was holding in her hand when she entered the hall. This paragraph had quite simply bewitched her. So it was in a voice filled with enthusiasm that she read to her uncles the above lines, which sung lyrically of the beauty of the Green Ray.

But what Miss Campbell did not tell them is that this same Green Ray was related to an old legend, whose innermost meaning she had not understood until then. It was one of the numerous inexplicable legends born in the Highlands, and affirms the following: this ray has the virtue of meaning that anyone who has seen it can no longer make a mistake in matters of sentiment; its appearance destroys illusions and lies. Those who have been lucky enough to see it once will see their own heart clearly as well as that of others.

May the young Highlander be forgiven the poetic credulity that the reading of this article in the *Morning Post* had revived in her imagination.

Whilst they listened to Miss Campbell, the brothers Sam and Sib looked at one another wide-eyed with a kind of stupefaction. They had lived up to then without seeing the Green Ray, and they thought that it was possible to survive without ever seeing it. But it appeared that this was not Helena's opinion. She intended to make the most important act of her life dependent on the observation of this unique phenomenon.

'Ah! Is that what is meant by the Green Ray?' said brother Sam, nodding his head gently.

'Yes', Miss Campbell replied.

'And you absolutely wish to see it?' said brother Sib.

'I will see it dear uncles, with your permission, and as soon as possible if you don't mind!'

'And what then, after you have seen it?'

'After I have seen it we can speak of Mr Aristobulus Ursiclos.'

Brother Sam and brother Sib exchanged a secret glance and smiled in a knowing manner.

'Then let's go and see this Green Ray', said one of them.

'Without a moment's delay!' added the other.

A movement from Miss Campbell's hand stopped them just as they were about to open the window of the hall.

'We must wait until the sun sets', she said.

'This evening then...' brother Sam replied.

'Until the sun sets over the purest of horizons', Miss Campbell added.

'Very well, after dinner we'll all three of us go to Rosneath Point', said brother Sib.

'Or we could simply climb up the tower', added brother Sam.

'The only view from both Rosneath Point and the tower is of the coast of the Clyde', replied Miss Campbell. 'But we must see the sun set over the sea. So take my advice, uncles, and take me to a place where I can see such a view as quickly as possible!'

Miss Campbell spoke so seriously, and smiled at them so prettily, that the Melville brothers were unable to resist a demand formulated in such a way.

Yet brother Sam still thought fit to observe, 'Perhaps it is not so very pressing?'

And brother Sib came to his aid, adding, 'We have plenty of time...'

Miss Campbell shook her head prettily. 'We don't have plenty of time,' she replied, 'and on the contrary, it is pressing!'

'Is that on account of Mr Aristobulus Ursiclos...' said brother Sam.

'Whose happiness, it appears, depends upon your observing the Green Ray...' said brother Sib.

'It is because we are already in the month of August, dear uncles!' Miss Campbell responded, 'and it will not be long before our Scottish sky is obscured by fog! It is because it is advisable to take advantage of the beautiful evenings left over to us at the end of summer and beginning of autumn! When shall we leave?'

What was certain was that if Miss Campbell was absolutely determined to see the Green Ray that year, there was no time to lose. They would have to travel immediately to some point of the Scottish coast that was exposed to the west, they would have to settle themselves there as comfortably as possible, go to watch the sunset every evening and then watch out for its last ray, and all this without even waiting another day. Perhaps then, with a bit of luck, should the sky lend itself to the observation of the phenomenon, which – as the *Morning Post* very rightly said – is a rare occurrence, Miss Campbell would see her somewhat fanciful desire fulfilled.

And that well-informed newspaper was right!

First of all, it was a question of finding and choosing a section of the west coast from which the phenomenon might be visible. Now in order to find such a place, they would have to leave behind the Firth of Clyde, due to the fact that its mouth is scattered with obstacles that limit how much can be seen from it. There are the Kyles of Bute, the Isle of Arran, the peninsulas of Knapdale and Kintyre, Jura, Islay, a vast scattering of rocks from the geological epoch that make a sort of archipelago of the entire western side of the county of Argyll. It was impossible to find a section of the horizon there where the sun could be seen setting over the sea.

So, if they did not wish to leave Scotland, they would have to go further north or further south to a place where the horizon was unbroken, and that before the misty autumn evenings set in.

To Miss Campbell it mattered little where they went. She was indifferent as to whether she was taken to the Irish coast, the French coast, the Norwegian coast, or the Spanish or Portuguese coast, so long as the radiant star, when it was setting, took its leave of her with its last rays, and, whether it were agreeable to the Melville brothers or not, they would have to follow her!

Her two uncles thus hastened to speak, though not before they had consulted one another with a glance. And what a glance it was, a glance enlivened by a touch of diplomatic delicacy!

'Well, my dear Helena,' said brother Sam, 'nothing can be easier than to satisfy you! Let's go to Oban.'

'It is obvious that we will find nowhere better than Oban', added brother Sib.

'Let us go to Oban,' Miss Campbell replied, 'but is there a marine horizon at Oban?'

'Is there a sea horizon!' cried brother Sam.

'There are more like two!' cried brother Sib.

'Very well, let's go!'

The country house in Helensburgh…

'In three days', said one of the uncles.

'In two days', said the other, judging it opportune to make this slight concession.

'No, tomorrow', Miss Campbell replied, rising from her seat as the dinner bell rang.

'Tomorrow...Yes...tomorrow!' added brother Sam.

'We wish we were there already!' replied brother Sib.

They were speaking the truth. And why this sudden hurry? It was because Aristobulus Ursiclos happened to have been on holiday in Oban for the last fortnight. And because Miss Campbell, who was unaware of this fact, would there find herself in the presence of the young man who had been chosen by the Melville brothers from among the most scholarly of men and moreover, although they scarcely suspected this, from among the most boring. And so, thought the two cunning individuals, after having fatigued her sight to no avail watching sunsets, Miss Campbell would give up her whim and would end up giving her hand to her fiancé. Even if Helena had suspected their plan, she would have been willing to set off all the same. The presence of Aristobulus Ursiclos was not calculated to annoy her.

'Bet!'

'Beth!'

'Bess!'

'Betsy!'

'Betty!'

The series of names echoed through the hall once again, but this time dame Bess appeared and received the order to be ready for immediate departure on the morrow.

They must indeed make haste, for the barometer was above thirty inches and three tenths (769 mm) and promised good weather for some time. If they left tomorrow morning, they would arrive in Oban early enough to watch the sunset.

Dame Bess and Partridge were naturally extremely busy that day with preparations for the departure. The housekeeper's forty-seven keys rattled in the pocket of her skirt like the bells on a Spanish mule. There were so many wardrobes and drawers to open and shut! The house at Helensburgh would perhaps be closed for a long time, for was it not necessary to reckon on Miss Campbell's whims? And supposing that charming individual wanted to chase after her Green Ray? And what if this Green Ray made a point of hiding? What would happen if the skyline at Oban failed to produce the purity necessary for this type of observation? What if they had to find another astronomical post on a more southerly coast of Scotland, England, Ireland, or indeed of Europe? It was agreed that they were to leave tomorrow, but when would they return? In a month, in six months, in a year, in ten years?

'What's behind this idea of seeing the Green Ray?' dame Bess asked Partridge, who was doing his best to help.

'I don't know,' Partridge replied, 'but it must be important, for our young mistress does nothing without good reason, as you well know, mavourneen.'

Mavourneen is an expression that is used freely in Scotland. It is almost the equivalent of the French 'ma chère', and so it did not displease the excellent housekeeper to be called such a name by the valiant Scot.

'Partridge,' she replied, 'I am of your opinion that there could well be some hidden secret behind this whim of Miss Campbell's, of which we had no suspicion.'

'What is it?'

'Ah! Who knows? Perhaps she plans to refuse, or at least to delay, her uncles' plans!'

'To tell the truth,' said Partridge, 'I don't understand why the masters are so besotted with Mr Ursiclos! Is he really the husband who will suit our young lady?'

'You may be certain Partridge,' replied dame Bess, 'that if he only half pleases her, she will not marry him. She will say no to her uncles in her pretty way and give them a kiss on each cheek, and they will be utterly surprised at having thought for one moment of this young suitor, whose claims I don't much care for.'

'Nor I, mavourneen.'

'You see Partridge, Miss Campbell's heart is like this drawer,

'You see Partridge...'

well closed and securely locked. She alone has the key, and, in order to open it, she must give it up...'

'Or you must take it from her!' added Partridge with a smile of approbation.

'No-one will take it from her unless she wants it to be taken!' dame Bess replied, 'And may the wind carry my hat up to the top of St Mungo's spire if ever our young lady marries this Mr Ursiclos!'

'A Southerner,' Partridge cried, 'who might have been born in Scotland, but who has always lived south of the Tweed!'

Dame Bess shook her head. These two Highlanders got on well together. They would scarcely allow that the Lowlands formed a part of their old Caledonia, and that despite all the treaties of Union. Therefore they were decidedly not in favour of the projected marriage. They hoped that Miss Campbell would do better. Propriety might be completely satisfied, but to them propriety did not seem enough.

'Ah, Partridge,' resumed dame Bess, 'the old Highland customs were the best. I think the customs of our ancient clans meant that marriages used to afford more happiness than they do today!'

'You've never spoken a truer word, mavourneen!' Partridge replied gravely. 'Marriages used to be based more on the heart and less on the purse! Money's all very well of course, but affection is better!'

'Yes Partridge, and people wanted to know each other well before they married above all! Do you recall what happened at St Olla's fair in Kirkwall? All the time it lasted, right from the beginning of August, the young people got together in couples, and these couples were called "the brother and sister of the first of August"! Brother and sister! Was that not a good way to prepare them to become husband and wife? And look, here we are on the exact day on which St Olla's fair used to start. May God bring it back!'

'May He answer your wish!' Partridge replied. 'Master Sam and master Sib themselves, had they formed an acquaintance with some good Scottish woman, would not have escaped matrimony, and Miss Campbell would now have two aunts!'

'I admit you're right, Partridge,' dame Bess replied, 'but you try pairing Miss Campbell and Mr Ursiclos off today, and may the Clyde flow upstream from Helensburgh to Glasgow if their association is not broken off in a week's time!'

Without dwelling upon the inconveniences that might arise from this familiarity, as authorised by the customs of Kirkwall which have now died out, we should merely state that facts may perhaps have proved dame Bess correct. But, after all, Miss Campbell and Aristobulus Ursiclos were not brother and sister of the first of August, and, if their marriage ever did take place, the fiancés would not have been able to get to know each other beforehand as they would have done had they gone through the test of St Olla's fair!

Be that as it may, fairs are established for the purpose of business, not for that of marriage. Thus we must leave dame Bess and Partridge to their regrets, and add only that they lost not a minute's time through their conversation.

The departure had been decided on. The holiday destination had been chosen. The two Melville brothers and Miss Campbell would figure in the fashionable newspapers under the rubric 'trips and holidays' as leaving tomorrow for the bathing resort of Oban. But how was the trip to be carried out? This question remained to be settled.

One of two routes can be chosen to reach the small town situated on the Sound of Mull about a hundred miles northwest of Glasgow.

The first route is by land via Bowling, Dumbarton and the right-hand bank of the Leven until you reach Balloch at the head of Loch Lomond. You then cross the most beautiful of the Scottish lakes with its thirty islands lying between its historic shores, overflowing with memories of the MacGregors and the MacFarlanes and in the heart of Rob Roy and Robert Bruce country, to reach Dalmally. From there, following a road that skirts around the side of the mountains, usually about half way up and overlooking fastflowing streams and fjords, the awe-struck tourist passes across the foothills of the Grampians in the midst of heather-covered glens scattered with firs, oaks, larch and birch, and finally descends on Oban, whose coast is as picturesque as any along the shores of the entire Atlantic.

It makes a charming excursion, and one that every traveller to Scotland has either taken or ought to take, but there is no view of the sea along it. Therefore the Melville brothers' suggestion to Miss Campbell that they take this route met with little success.

The second route is both by river and by sea. The traveller goes down the Clyde as far as the Firth to which it gives its name, navigates between the islands and isles that make this capricious archipelago look like the hand of an enormous skeleton spread over that part of the ocean, and then travels back up along the right side of the hand to the port of Oban. This was the route that attracted Miss Campbell; the charming country of Loch Lomond and Loch Katrine held no further secrets for her. Moreover, through the gaps between the islands, far out from the straits and the firths, there were snatches where a view of the west could be had with the sea making the horizon more pronounced. Well, at sunset during the last hour of the crossing, so long as the horizon was not veiled by drizzle, might they not be able to see this Green Ray which lasts for barely a fifth of a second?

'You must understand, uncle Sam,' said Miss Campbell, 'you must understand, uncle Sib. It takes but a moment! So once I have seen what I want to see, the trip will be over and it will be useless to go and stay in Oban.'

But that was exactly what the Melville brothers did not want. They wanted to stay in Oban for a while – we already know the reason why – and didn't really want the phenomenon to appear too quickly and spoil their plans.

Nevertheless, as Miss Campbell had the casting vote on the subject, and as she voted for the sea route, the latter was chosen in preference to the one over land.

'Hang this Green Ray!' said brother Sam when Helena had left the hall.

'And those who dreamt it up!' brother Sib replied.

4

Down the Clyde

VERY EARLY NEXT day, 2 August, Miss Campbell, accompanied by the Melville brothers and followed by Partridge and dame Bess, got on the train at Helensburgh railway station. They had to travel to Glasgow to take the steamer, as it did not call anywhere along that part of the coast during its daily journey from the metropolis to Oban.

At seven o'clock the train deposited the five travellers on the arrival platform in Glasgow, and a carriage conducted them to Broomielaw Bridge.

There the *Columba* paddle steamer was awaiting its passengers. Black smoke bellowed out of its two chimneys and mingled with the still thick fog that hung over the Clyde. This morning haze was however beginning to disappear, and the leaden disk of the sun was already showing a few hints of gold. It was the start of a beautiful day.

Miss Campbell and her companions embarked immediately after seeing their luggage put on board.

At that moment the bell made its third and final call to late-comers, then the engineer brought the engine to life, the paddle wheels moved backwards and forwards creating large yellowy bubbles, a long whistle sounded, the moorings were cast off and the *Columba* sailed quickly away with the current.

It would be bad form for tourists in the United Kingdom to complain. The boats that the transport companies place at their disposal everywhere are magnificent. There are few stretches of water too slight, few lakes too small, and few gulfs too inferior as not to be crossed each day by elegant steamers. It is thus not surprising that the Clyde is among the most favoured in this respect. So there were vast numbers of steamers stationed on the slipways along the Broomielaw Quay, their paddle drums painted in the very brightest colours, gold vying with vermilion, constantly letting off steam and ready to set off in all directions.

The *Columba* was no exception to the rule. She was very long and fast with a very slender bow. She followed her lane expertly, and was equipped with a powerful engine that drove wheels of a large diameter; she was a boat that sailed well. Inside there was every possible comfort in her lounges and dining rooms. On the vast spar deck, which was sheltered by an awning with light lambrequins, were benches and seats covered with soft cushions, forming a real terrace surrounded by an elegant guardrail, where the passengers found themselves in the midst of beautiful views and fresh air.

There was no lack of passengers. They came from all around, from England as well as from Scotland. The month of August is, par excellence, the month for excursions, and those on the Clyde or to the Hebrides are particularly sought after. There were whole families there, whose union God had generously blessed. There were lively young girls, calm young men, children already used to the wonders of travelling, pastors, who are always to be found in great numbers on board steamers, with high silk hats on their heads, long black frock coats with upright collars and white ties showing above the neck of their waistcoats. Then there were several farmers in Scottish bonnets, whose somewhat serious air recalled the old 'bonnet lairds' of some sixty years before, and finally there were half a dozen foreigners: Germans who have an air of importance even when they are not in Germany, and two or three Frenchmen who never give up their air of genial amiability, even when they are no longer in France.

If Miss Campbell had resembled most of her compatriots, who sit down in some corner as soon as they have embarked and do not move for the entire journey, she would only have seen the banks of the Clyde in so far as they passed before her eyes without

Broomielaw Bridge, Glasgow

turning her head. But she liked to walk up and down the steamer, sometimes towards the bow, sometimes towards the stern, looking at the towns, market towns, villages and hamlets with which the banks of the Clyde are scattered incessantly. The consequence of this was that brother Sam and brother Sib, who accompanied her, replying to her comments, approving her observations and confirming her remarks, did not have an hour's rest between Glasgow and Oban. Moreover, they did not dream of complaining, as it was part of their duty as bodyguards, and they followed instinctively, exchanging several good pinches of snuff, which kept them in good humour.

Dame Bess and Partridge, having taken seats towards the front of the spar deck, talked amicably of past times, of lost customs and of old clans in a state of disarray. Where had those good old days disappeared to? At that time the clear horizons of the Clyde were not hidden behind the coal smoke spewing out of factories, its banks did not ring with the muffled blows of power hammers, its calm waters were never disturbed by a power output equivalent to that of several thousand horse power!

'Those times will return, and perhaps sooner than we might think!' said dame Bess in a tone of conviction.

'I hope so,' Partridge replied gravely, 'and with them we will find the old customs of our ancestors!'

Meanwhile, the banks of the Clyde were moving rapidly from the bow of the *Columba* to her stern, like the images in a moving panorama. On the right appeared the village of Partick, located at the mouth of the Kelvin, with its great docks, which were destined for the construction of iron ships, facing those of Govan, which are situated on the opposite bank. How many rattling noises there were, and how many curls of smoke and steam, and how displeasing it all was to the eyes and ears of Partridge and his companion!

But little by little all this industrial din and sooty smog would cease. The yards, covered slipways, high factory chimneys and gigantic iron scaffolds, which looked like the cages in a menagerie for mastodons, were replaced by pretty dwellings, cottages buried in trees and Anglo-Saxon-style villas scattered on green hills. It was as if an unbroken succession of country houses and castles unfolded from one town to the next.

After the ancient royal market town of Renfrew, situated on the left-hand bank of the river, the wooded hills of Kilpatrick emerged on the right above the village of the same name, which no Irishman can pass without removing his hat for it was there that St Patrick, the patron saint of Ireland, was born.

The Clyde, which had been a river up to that point, then began to turn into a true arm of the sea. Dame Bess and Partridge saluted the ruins of Dunglass Castle, which brought to mind some old memories of Scottish history, but they averted their eyes when they passed the obelisk raised in honour of Henry Bell, the inventor of the first steamboat to disturb the peaceful waters with its paddlewheels.

Several miles further on, the tourists, their Murray in hand, gazed at Dumbarton Castle, which towers up at a height of over 500 feet on its basalt rock. The more elevated of the two summits still bears the name of Wallace's Seat after one of the heroes in the battles for independence.

At that moment, a gentleman thought fit to give a short historical lecture from the top of the bridge in order to educate his fellow passengers. No-one had asked him to do so, but nor did anyone think of objecting. Half an hour later, not a single passenger on board the *Columba,* unless they were deaf, could possibly have been ignorant of the fact that it was highly probable that the Romans had fortified Dumbarton, that the historic rock had been transformed into a royal fortress at the beginning of the eighteenth century, that under the Act of Union it was one of four places in the kingdom of Scotland that could not be dismantled, that it was from this port that Mary Stuart left for France, where she was to be made 'queen for a day' through her marriage with François II, in 1548, and finally that Napoleon was to have been held there in 1815 until the minister Castlereagh resolved to imprison him on St Helena instead.

'That was very instructive,' said brother Sam.

'Instructive and interesting,' replied brother Sib, 'this gentleman deserves to be praised!'

Dumbarton Castle...

In fact, the two uncles had not dreamed of missing a single word of the lecture. They thus expressed their satisfaction to the impromptu professor.

Miss Campbell, who was absorbed in her own reflections, had heard nothing of this well-known history lesson. She was not interested in it, at least not at that moment. She did not even look at the ruins of Cardross castle on the right-hand side of the river, where Robert the Bruce had died. Her eyes searched in vain for a marine horizon, though they would not be able to see one until the *Columba* had got free of the succession of banks, promontories and hills that bound the Firth of Clyde. Moreover, the steamer then passed before the small town of Helensburgh – Port Glasgow, the ruins of Newark Castle and the peninsula of Rosneath – it was the same view that the young lady of the manor saw each day from the windows of the mansion. So she began to wonder whether the steamer was not sailing up the stream that wound through the park.

And, further on, why should her thoughts be carried away in the midst of the hundreds of ships that crowded the docks at Greenock at the mouth of the river? What did it matter to her that the immortal Watt had been born in this town of forty thousand inhabitants, which is like the industrial and commercial ante-chamber of Glasgow? Why, three miles further downstream, should she stop to look at the village of Gourock on the left and at the village of Dunoon on the right, and at the winding and jagged fjords that bite so deeply into the headlands of Argyll, indented like a part of the Norwegian coast?

No! Miss Campbell was looking out impatiently for the ruin of Leven Tower. Did she expect to see some goblin appear there? Not in the least, but she did want to be the first to point out Cloch Lighthouse, which signals the end of the Firth of Clyde.

The lighthouse finally appeared, like a gigantic lamp, where the shore bent away.

'Cloch, uncle Sam,' she said, 'Cloch, Cloch!'

'Yes, Cloch,' brother Sam replied with the precision of a Highland echo.

'The sea, uncle Sib!'

'Indeed, the sea,' replied brother Sib.

'How beautiful it is!' repeated the two uncles.

You would have been forgiven for thinking that it was the first time they had ever seen it!

There was no mistaking it. There was indeed a marine horizon at the entrance to the Firth.

However, the sun was not yet halfway through its daytime course. At least seven hours would have to pass at the fifty-sixth parallel before it disappeared beneath the waves – seven hours of impatience for Miss Campbell! Moreover, this horizon was to the southwest, that's to say at a section of the arc that the radiant star only skims across at the time of the winter solstice. Therefore, there was not the place to look for the appearance of the phenomenon. It would be more to the west, and even slightly to the north, as the early part of August precedes the September equinox by six weeks.

But that mattered little. It was the sea that now stretched before Miss Campbell's eyes. Between the islands of Cumbrae, beyond the large Isle of Bute, whose outline was softened by a slight haze, beyond the small crests of Ailsa Craig and the mountains of Arran, the line separating the sky and water could be seen on the open ocean as distinctly as if it had been drawn with a ruler.

Miss Campbell was watching it all. She was completely absorbed in her thoughts and said not a word. As she stood upright and immobile on the bridge, the sun cast her much shortened shadow at her feet. She seemed to be measuring the length of the arc that still separated it from the point at which its radiant disc would drown itself in the waters of the Hebridean archipelago… in the hope that the sky, which was so clear at that moment, was not obscured by crepuscular haze!

A voice roused the young dreamer from her reverie.

'It is time,' said brother Sib.

'Time? Time for what, dear uncles?'

'Time for lunch,' said brother Sam.

'Let's go then,' replied Miss Campbell.

5

From One Boat to the Next

AFTER PARTAKING OF an excellent Scottish lunch, which consisted of both cold and hot dishes, in the dining room of the *Columba*, Miss Campbell and her uncles went back up on deck.

Helena could not hold back a cry of disappointment when she again took up her place on the spar deck.

'My horizon has gone!' she said.

It must be confessed her horizon was no longer there. It had disappeared some minutes before. The steamer, heading northwards, was at that moment making its way back up the long strait of the Kyles of Bute.

'This is too bad, uncle Sam!' said Miss Campbell with a little pout of reproach.

'But my dear girl...'

'I will remember this, uncle Sib!'

The two brothers did not know what to say, and yet it was certainly not their fault if the *Columba* had changed her course and was then heading towards the northwest.

Indeed, there are two very different routes by which to get to Oban from Glasgow by sea.

The longer route was the one that the *Columba* had not taken. Having called at Rothesay, the principal town on the Isle of Bute, which is dominated by its ancient eleventh-century castle and sheltered on the western side by high hills that protect it from the gales coming in off the open sea, the steamer can continue down the Firth of Clyde, then make its way along the eastern coast of the isle, passing in sight of both Great Cumbrae and Little Cumbrae and advancing in that direction as far as the southern tip of the Isle of Arran, which belongs almost entirely to the Duke of Hamilton from the base of its rocks to the summit of Goatfell at almost eight hundred metres above sea-level. Then, the helmsman turns the helm, the compass is set to a westerly bearing, the ship rounds the Isle of Arran and then the large finger of the Kintyre peninsula, it then heads back up the western coast, plunges into the Sound of Gigha, passes between the islands of Islay and Jura, and arrives at the wide entrance to the Firth of Lorn, which becomes increasingly narrow until it closes a little above Oban.

In short, if Miss Campbell had some right to complain that the *Columba* had not taken that route, perhaps her uncles too had cause to regret it. Indeed, had they passed along the coast of Islay, they would have seen the former residence of the MacDonalds, who, at the start of the seventeenth century, had been conquered and driven out by the Campbells. Seeing the scene of this historical event, which touched them so closely, would have set the hearts of the Melville brothers, not to mention dame Bess and Partridge, beating in unison.

As for Miss Campbell, the much regretted horizon would have been visible for a longer period of time. Indeed, from the tip of Arran to the Mull of Kintyre, the view of the sea is to the south. From the Mull of Kintyre to the end of Islay, the view to the west is of the immense stretch of ocean bounded only by the American coast three thousand miles away.

But that route is long and sometimes troublesome, if not dangerous, and it was necessary to consider those tourists who might be frightened by the eventualities of a crossing that is often rendered inclement by a somewhat heavy swell off the shores of the Hebrides.

Several engineers – small-time Lesseps – have had the thought of turning the Kintyre peninsula into an island and, thanks to their work, the Crinan Canal has been cut through its northern part. It shortens the journey by at least two hundred miles, and only three to four hours are needed to pass through it.

This was the route that the *Columba* was taking to sail from

Glasgow to Oban, between the lochs and the straits, the only view being of banks, forests and mountains. Of all the passengers, Miss Campbell was undoubtedly the only one to regret the loss of the other itinerary, but she had to resign herself to it. Moreover, would not her marine horizon become visible again a little beyond the Crinan canal, only a few hours later and well before the sun's disc brushed against its surface?

As the tourists who had lingered behind in the dining room came back up on deck, the *Columba* was passing close by the small island of Eilean Greig at the entrance to Loch Riddon, the last fortress where the heroic Duke of Argyll, who was crushed in the fight for the political and religious freedom of Scotland, took refuge before going to Edinburgh, where he was beheaded by the blade of the Scottish guillotine. Then the steamer veered south and descended the Kyles of Bute in the midst of that wonderful panorama of arid and wooded isles, whose rough outlines were rendered indistinct by a light mist. Finally, after rounding Ardlamont Point, it headed back in a northerly direction through Loch Fyne, leaving the village of East Tarbert on the coast of Kintyre behind on its left-hand side, sailed around Ardrishaig Point and reached the entrance to the Crinan Canal in the village of Ardrishaig.

There they had to leave the *Columba*, as she was too big to travel down the canal, whose incline is atoned for by fifteen locks and which only admits narrow vessels with a shallow draught to navigate its nine miles.

A small steamer, the *Linnet,* was awaiting the *Columba*'s passengers. The transfer was effected in a few minutes. Everyone was installed on the steamer's spar deck, somewhat ill at ease, and then the *Linnet* sped quickly between the banks of the canal, while a bagpiper, dressed in national dress, played his instrument. There is nothing as melancholic as those strange songs, supported by the monotonous bass tones of three drones, which only use the intervals of a major scale in which the leading-note is missing, as in the old airs from former centuries.

It is a charming journey. In places the canal passes between high banks, sometimes it skirts the sides of hills covered with

The strait of the Kyles of Bute.

heather, here it traverses open countryside and there it is contained between the confined walls of reaches. There is some delay in the locks. Whilst the lock keepers quickly lock the boat, local youths, girls and children come and politely offer fresh milk to the tourists, speaking with that Gaelic idiom that the Celts used to use, which is often incomprehensible, even to the Scot.

Six hours later – there had been a two hour delay at a lock that was not working properly – they had got past the hamlets and farms of this somewhat dreary region and the immense bogs beside the River Add, which extend along the right-hand side of the canal. The *Linnet* stopped shortly after the village of Bellanoch. A second transfer took place. The passengers of the *Columba* became the passengers of the *Glengarry*. They headed in a north-westerly direction, leaving Crinan Bay and rounding the point on which the ancient feudal castle of Duntrune stands.

They had not seen a marine horizon since the glimpse they had had when rounding the Isle of Bute.

It is easy to imagine how impatient Miss Campbell was. On these waters, which were bounded in every direction, she might have been in the heart of Scotland, amongst the lochs in the midst of Rob Roy country. There were picturesque islands everywhere with their gentle undulations and their plantations of birch and larch.

Finally the *Glengarry* passed the northern tip of Jura and, between this point and the island of Scarba, the sea and the sky met.

'There it is, my dear Helena!' said brother Sam, pointing towards the west.

'It was not our fault that those cursed islands, may the Devil confound them, hid it from you for a while!' added brother Sib.

'You are completely forgiven, uncles,' Miss Campbell replied, 'but don't let it happen again!'

6

The Gulf of Corryvreckan

IT WAS THEN six in the evening and the sun had as yet only covered four fifths of its course. The *Glengarry* would most certainly arrive in Oban before the day star sank into the waters of the Atlantic. Miss Campbell thus had some grounds for thinking that her wishes would be granted that very evening. In fact the cloudless sky seemed expressly made for observing the phenomenon, and the marine horizon ought to remain visible between the islands of Oronsay, Colonsay and Mull for the last part of the crossing.

But a very unexpected incident was to delay the progress of the steamer somewhat.

Miss Campbell, possessed by her obsession, remained immobile, never losing sight of the circular line between the two islands. Where the sky and sea met, the reflection produced a silver triangle, the last shades of which died away at the side of the *Glengarry*.

Miss Campbell was undoubtedly the only person on board whose eyes were obstinately fixed on that part of the horizon. She was thus the only one who noticed how choppy the sea seemed to be between the headland and the island of Scarba. At the same time, she heard the faraway sound of waves crashing together. However, the breeze raised scarcely any ripples in the water through which the steamer's stem was cutting and which was so calm as to appear almost viscous.

'What is causing all that noise and turmoil?' Miss Campbell asked her uncles.

The Melville brothers were unable to answer her, knowing no

more than she herself did what was happening three miles away in the narrow strait.

Miss Campbell then turned to the captain of the *Glengarry*, who was walking on the bridge, and asked him what was causing the water to be so rough and loud.

'A simple tidal phenomenon,' the captain replied, 'what you are hearing is the sound of the Gulf of Corryvreckan.'

'But the weather is wonderful,' observed Miss Campbell, 'and the breeze is hardly perceptible!'

'This phenomenon is not dependent on the weather', the captain replied. 'It is an effect of the rising sea, which, when it leaves the Sound of Jura, finds no other outlet than between the islands of Jura and Scarba. That's why the incoming tide rushes in with such extreme violence. It would be extremely dangerous for a small boat to venture into it.'

The Gulf of Corryvreckan is feared in the area, and with good reason. It is listed as one of the most curious places in the Hebridean archipelago. It could perhaps be compared to the Raz de Sein off the coast of Brittany, formed by the narrowing of the sea between the embankment of the same name and the baie des Trépassés, and to the Raz Blanchart between Alderney and Cherbourg, through which the waters of the English Channel flow. Legend has it that it owes its name to a Scandinavian prince whose ship perished there in Celtic times. In reality, it is a dangerous passage into which many boats have been dragged at their peril, and whose currents may be compared to the sinister maelstrom off the Norwegian coast.

However, Miss Campbell continued to watch the violent seething of the water, and her attention was drawn to one point of the strait in particular. You might have been forgiven for thinking that there was a rock in the centre of the channel, had the mass not been moving up and down with the undulations of the swell.

'Look captain! Look!' said Miss Campbell, 'If it isn't a rock, then what is it?'

'It must be a wreck that's been dragged along by the currents,' the captain replied, 'unless…'

He picked up his telescope. 'A boat!' he cried.

All eyes were fixed on that single spot...

'A boat!' repeated Miss Campbell.

'Yes... it has to be... a rowing boat in distress on the waters of Corryvreckan!'

At the captain's words, the passengers immediately made their way onto the bridge. They looked in the direction of the gulf. There could no longer be any doubt that a boat had been dragged into the channel and that, carried along by the currents of the rising tide and caught up in the swirling waters, she was heading towards certain destruction.

All eyes were fixed on that single spot in the gulf, four or five miles from the *Glengarry*.

'It is probably only a rowing boat adrift,' observed one of the passengers.

'No it isn't! I can see a man,' replied another.

'A man... no, two men!' cried Partridge, who had come to stand next to Miss Campbell.

There were indeed two men and they were no longer in control of the boat. The slight breeze off the land was not enough to enable their sail to draw them out of the eddy, and oars would have proved ineffective against the pull of Corryvreckan.

'Captain!' Miss Campbell cried. 'We can't let those poor men perish! They're lost if we leave them! We have to go to their rescue! We have to!'

Everyone on board thought the same and they all awaited the captain's response.

'The *Glengarry*,' he said, 'can't venture into the middle of Corryvreckan! But perhaps, if we go nearer, we may be able to get within reach of the boat!'

Turning towards the passengers, he seemed to await their approbation.

Miss Campbell went towards him.

'We must, captain! We must!' she cried ardently. 'My fellow passengers wish to as much as I do! It's a matter of life or death for two men, whom you may be able to save... Oh captain! I beg you!'

'Yes! Yes!' cried some of the passengers, moved by the young girl's warm intervention.

The captain took up his telescope again, and looked closely in the direction of the currents in the channel. Then he addressed the man at the helm, who was stood close by on the bridge.

'Pay attention!' he said. 'Helm to starboard!'

Under the influence of the helm, the steamer veered west. The engineer received the order to increase her steam and the *Glengarry* quickly left behind the headland of the island of Jura on the left.

Nobody on board spoke. All eyes were anxiously fixed on the boat, which steadily became more visible.

She was only a small fishing boat, whose mast had been lowered in order to avoid the effects of the jolts caused by the violent impact of the waves.

One of the two men in the boat was lying stretched out at the back, the other, rowing with all his might, was trying to extricate her from the centre of the swell. If he failed, they would both be lost.

Half an hour later the *Glengarry* arrived at the edge of Corryvreckan, and began to pitch violently on the first waves. But no-one on board complained, even though the speed of the current was of the sort that might well have frightened mere tourists.

Indeed, at that part of the strait the water was completely white, requiring the sails to be reefed. All that could be seen was a vast layer of foam, which was whipped up into enormous masses when the waters collided with the shallow bed.

The rowing boat was now only half a mile away. The man bending over the oars was making a supreme effort to get her out of the eddy. He knew that the *Glengarry* was coming to help them, but he also knew that the steamer would not be able to advance much further, and that it was up to him to reach her. His companion, who remained motionless in the stern, seemed to be devoid of all feeling.

Miss Campbell, victim to the strongest emotions, never took her eyes off this boat in distress, which she had been the first to point out on the waters of the gulf, and towards which, thanks to her instantaneous plea, the *Glengarry* was now heading.

However, the situation got worse. They began to fear that the steamer would not arrive in time. She was moving only very slowly now so as to avoid any serious damage, but she was shipping water at the front and the waves were already threatening to reach the openwork of the stokehold, whose fire they were quite capable of extinguishing – a formidable eventuality in these rapid currents.

The captain, leaning upon the handrail of the bridge, was watching to make sure that they didn't drift away from their course, and was manoeuvring the steamer skilfully to ensure that she didn't turn abeam.

But the rowing boat could not free herself from the eddies. At times she would disappear all of a sudden behind an enormous breaker, at others, seized by the concentric currents of the gulf, whose speed grew in proportion to their radius, she spun round in a circle with the rapidity of an arrow, or rather of a stone spinning from the end of a catapult.

'Faster! Faster!' Miss Campbell repeated, no longer able to contain herself.

But at the sight of these swirling masses, some of the passengers were already beginning to scream with fear. The captain, who was aware of the responsibility he was taking on, hesitated as to whether they should continue their course through the Corryvreckan channel.

And yet the distance between the rowing boat and the *Glengarry* was now barely half a cable length, or three hundred feet, and thus it was easy to make out the two unfortunate men who were being carried to their deaths.

They were an old sailor and a young man. The former was lying at the rear of the boat; the latter was fighting at the oars.

At that moment a violent wave assailed the steamer, putting her in a somewhat difficult position.

The captain could not advance any further into the channel, and it was with great difficulty that he used the wheel to manoeuvre the steamer and keep her upright in the current.

All of a sudden, after tottering for a moment on the crest of a wave, the small boat slid sideways and disappeared.

Everyone onboard gave a shout of horror!

Had the boat sunk? No. It rose again on the back of another wave, and one final effort with the oars brought her alongside the steamer.

'Get to it! Get to it!' cried the sailors in the bow.

And they caught up a coil of ropes, watching out for the moment to throw them.

Suddenly the captain, seeing a slight improvement between two swells, gave the order to increase steam. The speed of the *Glengarry* increased and she ventured boldly between the two islands, whilst the fishing boat gained a few more fathoms.

The ropes were thrown out, seized, and tied around the foot of the mast. Then the engines of the *Glengarry* were put in reverse to enable her to get away more quickly, the small boat at her side following in tow.

At that moment the young man, abandoning his oars, lifted his companion in his arms, and, with the help of the sailors from the steamer, the old seaman was hoisted on board. He had been knocked down by a heavy swell whilst the boat had been dragged along in the channel, and had thus been unable to help the young man, who had been left to depend entirely on his own efforts.

The latter had just sprung onto the bridge of the *Glengarry*. He had lost none of his self-possession, his face was calm and his entire bearing showed that both moral and physical courage came naturally to him.

Straightaway he busied himself with looking after his companion, who was the owner of the fishing boat and who was quickly brought around by a good glass of brandy.

'Mr Oliver!' he said.

'Ah, my old sailor,' said the young man, 'so, what do you think of this heavy swell?'

'It's nothing! I've seen many the like of it! It's passing already!'

'Yes, thank Heaven! But my imprudence and my desire to get closer and closer nearly cost us dear... nevertheless here we are safe and sound!'

'And by your efforts, Mr Olivier!'

'No, with God's help!'

And the young man, clasping the old sailor to his chest, made no attempt to conceal his emotion, thereby winning over those who witnessed the scene.

Then, turning to the captain of the *Glengarry* as the latter came down off the bridge, he said, 'Captain, I don't know how to thank you for the service you've rendered us...'

'I merely carried out my duty, sir, and, to tell the truth, my passengers have more right to your gratitude than I do.'

The young man shook the captain's hand warmly, and then, taking off his hat, he bowed to the passengers gracefully.

Had not the *Glengarry* arrived, he and his companion would certainly have been dragged into the centre of Corryvreckan and lost.

Yet during this exchange of polite remarks and gestures, Miss Campbell had thought fit to withdraw into the background. She didn't want any attention to be drawn to the part that she had played in the outcome of this dramatic rescue. She was thus standing on the bow of the bridge, when, all of a sudden, her imagination appeared to come back to life and, turning back to face the west, the following words escaped her lips: 'What about the ray... and the sun?'

'The sun is no more!' said brother Sam.

'Our chance of seeing the ray has passed!' said brother Sib.

It was too late. The sun had already disappeared beneath a remarkably clear horizon, and had shot forth its Green Ray into space! But at that moment Miss Campbell's thoughts had been elsewhere, her eyes had been distracted, and the opportunity, which might perhaps be a long time in recurring, had been missed!

'What a pity!' she murmured, though without too much disappointment, as she through over everything that had just happened.

In the meantime, the *Glengarry* made her way out of the Gulf of Corryvreckan and resumed her northerly course. After shaking his companion's hand one last time, the old sailor then got back into his boat and set sail for the island of Jura.

As for the young man, his leather portmanteau or 'dorlach'

'Ah, my old sailor, my imprudence nearly cost us dear…!'

had been put on board and he made one extra tourist for the *Glengarry* to take to Oban.

Leaving behind the isles of Shuna and Luing on her right-hand side, on which the rich slate quarries belonging to the Marquis of Breadalbane are being dug, the steamer sailed alongside the island of Seil, which shelters this part of the Scottish coast, and soon afterwards, entering the Sound of Kerrera, she sailed between the volcanic island of Kerrera and the mainland. Then, as the twilight faded away, she made fast at the landing stage in the port of Oban.

7

Aristobulus Ursiclos

EVEN IF OBAN HAD attracted such a large throng of bathers to its beaches as do the busy bathing resorts of Brighton, Margate and Ramsgate, a person with the merits of Aristobulus Ursiclos could not have passed unnoticed.

Although not equal to its rivals, Oban is much sought after as a bathing resort by men and women of leisure in the United Kingdom. Its situation on the Sound of Mull, sheltered from the westerly winds by the isle of Kerrera, attracts many visitors. Some come to bathe in its healthy waters; others see it as a central base from which trips to Glasgow, Inverness and the most interesting of the Hebridean islands leave. Here it must be added that Oban is not, as so many other bathing resorts are, always full of invalids; most of the people who go there to spend the hot summer months are in good health, and so there is no risk, as there is in some spa towns, of playing whist with two invalids and one 'corpse'.

Oban is only around one hundred and fifty years old. Thus, in the layout of its squares, the arrangement of its houses and the construction of its roads, it has a completely modern character. However the church, a sort of Norman building with a pretty steeple; the old ivy-covered castle of Dunolly, which stands on a separate rock to the north of the town; its panorama of white houses and multi-coloured villas, which are set out in rows on the hills in the background; and lastly the tranquil waters of its bay, where elegant pleasure yachts are anchored, make for a picturesque view.

That year, and that particular August, there was no lack

of visitors, tourists and bathers in the small town of Oban. Amongst other names more or less illustrious, that of Aristobulus Ursiclos of Dumfries (Scottish Lowlands) might have been read in the register of one of the best hotels for several weeks already.

He was an 'individual' of twenty-eight years of age, who had never been young and would probably never be old. He had evidently been born at the age which he would appear to be throughout his life. His bearing was neither good nor bad, his face insignificant with hair that was too fair for a man. He was shortsighted and wore glasses; his nose was short and didn't seem to fit his face. Of the one hundred and thirty thousand hairs that every human head should possess, according to the latest statistics, he had barely sixty thousand left. A beard framed his cheeks and chin, giving him a face that looked somewhat like a monkey's. Had he been a monkey, he would have been a beautiful specimen – perhaps the missing link in the Darwinian scale connecting animals and humanity.

Aristobulus Ursiclos had lots of money and even more ideas. For a young scholar, he had had too much education, and only managed to weary others with his universal knowledge. He was a graduate of the universities of Oxford and Edinburgh, and had more knowledge of physics, chemistry, astronomy and mathematics than of literature. He was very pretentious, yet it did little but to make him look a fool. His chief mania, or his monomania if you like, was to give, at random, an explanation for anything that could be said to be natural; he was a sort of pedant and a disagreeable acquaintance. People didn't laugh at him because he was not laughable, but perhaps they did laugh at him because he was ridiculous. There could not have been a candidate less worthy of appropriating the motto of the English freemasons, *Audi, vide, tace,* than this artificial young man. He didn't listen, he saw nothing, and he was never silent. In a word, to borrow a comparison that is not inappropriate in the land of Walter Scott, Aristobulus Ursiclos, with his unqualified industrialism, was infinitely more like the bailie Nicol Jarvie than his poetical cousin Rob Roy MacGregor.

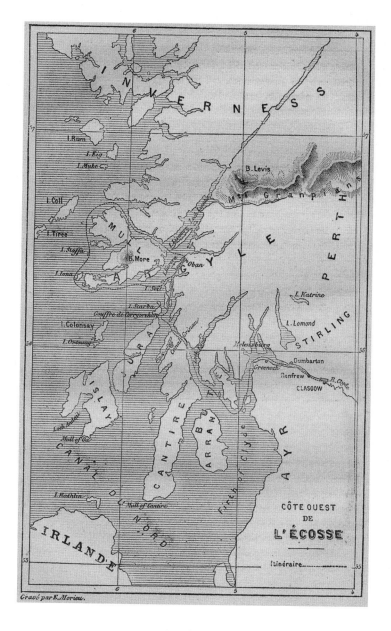

And what daughter of the Highlands, not excepting Miss Campbell, would not have preferred Rob Roy to Nicol Jarvie?

Such was Aristobulus Ursiclos. How could the Melville brothers have become infatuated with this pedant to the point of wanting to make him their nephew-in-law? How had he made himself agreeable to these sexagenarians? Perhaps it was simply because he was the first to have made them an overture of this kind in relation to their niece. Brother Sam and brother Sib had undoubtedly said to one another with a kind of naïve delight:

Here's a rich young man from a good family, with a large fortune, which he has inherited from his parents and relations, and moreover, who is extraordinarily well educated! It would be an excellent match for our dear Helena! This is a marriage that will go very smoothly, and it is quite proper since we are agreed on it!'

At that point, they had treated themselves to a good pinch of snuff, and then shut the communal snuffbox with a sharp little snap that seemed to say:

'That's that!'

The Melville brothers thus thought they had been very clever in bringing Miss Campbell to Oban, thanks to her strange whim in relation to the Green Ray. Without it appearing that it had been planned, she would be able to resume the meetings with Aristobulus Ursiclos, which had been momentarily interrupted due to his absence.

The Melville brothers and Miss Campbell had exchanged their residence in Helensburgh for the most beautiful apartments in the Caledonian Hotel. If their stay in Oban should continue, it would perhaps be appropriate to rent a villa on the hills overlooking the town, but, meanwhile, with the help of dame Bess and Partridge, they were all comfortably installed in the establishment belonging to Mr MacFyne. They would see later.

It was thus from the vestibule of the Caledonian Hotel, situated on the seafront, almost opposite the landing stage, that the Melville brothers emerged at nine in the morning, the day after their arrival. Miss Campbell was still resting in her room on the first floor, little suspecting that her uncles were going to look for Aristobulus Ursiclos.

The inseparable pair went down to the beach, and, knowing that their 'suitor' was staying in one of the hotels on the north side of the bay, they headed in that direction.

It must be admitted that they were guided by a sort of premonition. Ten minutes after they had set out, Aristobulus Ursiclos, who was taking his usual morning walk, following the latest movements of the tide in pursuit of science, met them and exchanged with them one of those handshakes that is commonplace and purely automatic.

'Mr Ursiclos!' said the Melville brothers.

'Gentlemen!' responded Aristobulus in that affected tone of voice that feigns surprise. 'You gentlemen... here... in Oban?'

'Since yesterday evening!' said brother Sam.

'And we are happy, Mr Ursiclos, to see you looking so well,' said brother Sib.

'Oh, very well indeed, gentlemen – you've no doubt heard of the telegram that has just arrived?'

'The telegram?' said brother Sam. 'Has Gladstone already...?'

'It has nothing to do with Gladstone,' Aristobulus Ursiclos responded somewhat scornfully. 'It is a meteorological telegram.'

'Ah, indeed!' the two uncles replied.

'Yes! It announces that the depression at Swinemünde has headed north and is swelling noticeably. Its centre is now near Stockholm, where the barometer has fallen by an inch or twenty five millimetres – to employ the decimal system used by scientists – and now stands at only twenty-eight inches and six tenths, or seven hundred and twenty-six millimetres. Though the atmospheric pressure in England and Scotland is varying very little, it fell by a tenth yesterday in Valentia and two tenths in Stornaway.'

'And what of this depression...?' asked brother Sam.

'What are we to conclude from it?' added brother Sib.

'That this fine weather will not last,' replied Aristobulus Ursiclos, 'and that the sky will soon become charged with wind from the south-west and will bring in haze from the North Atlantic.'

The Melville brothers thanked the young scientist for having acquainted them with this interesting forecast, and concluded from it that they might have to wait some time for the Green Ray. They were not particularly annoyed by this, as the delay would prolong their stay in Oban.

'And what brings you here, gentlemen…?' asked Aristobulus Ursiclos, after picking up a flint, which he examined with great attention.

The two uncles took care not to interrupt him during this study, but when the flint had been added to the collection already in the young scholar's pocket, brother Sib said, 'We have come with the very natural design of spending some time here.'

'And we should add,' said brother Sam, 'that Miss Campbell has accompanied us here…'

'Ah, Miss Campbell!' replied Aristobulus Ursiclos. 'I believe that this flint is from the Gaelic epoch. There are some traces… really, I would be delighted to see Miss Campbell again… traces of meteoric iron. This climate, which is remarkably mild, will do her a great deal of good.'

'She is very well anyway', observed brother Sam, 'and doesn't need to recover her health.'

'No matter', replied Aristobulus Ursiclos. 'The air here is excellent. Twenty-one percent oxygen and seventy-nine percent nitrogen with a little water vapour in a quantity that is healthy. As for carbon dioxide, there are hardly any traces of it. I analyse it every morning.'

The Melville brothers decided to view this as an amiable attention addressed to Miss Campbell.

'But,' asked Aristobulus Ursiclos, 'if you did not come to Oban on account of your health, gentlemen, may I ask why you left your home in Helensburgh?'

'We have no need to hide the reason from you given the situation in which we find ourselves…' replied brother Sam.

'Am I to see in this move,' resumed the young scholar, interrupting his words, 'the desire, moreover a very natural one, to

Then, turning to the captain…

have me meet Miss Campbell in circumstances in which we can get to know one another better, that is to say to appreciate one another?'

'Certainly,' replied brother Sam. 'We thought that, in this way, our goal might be attained more quickly…'

'I approve, gentlemen', said Aristobulus Ursiclos. 'Here, on neutral territory, Miss Campbell and I may, on occasion, speak of the fluctuations of the sea, of the direction of the wind, of the height of the waves, of the variation in the tides and of other physical phenomena that are sure to interest her to a high degree!'

After exchanging a smile of satisfaction, the Melville brothers bowed their approbation. They added that, when they returned to their country house in Helensburgh, they would be happy to receive their amiable guest on a more permanent basis.

Aristobulus Ursiclos replied that he would be all the happier to visit them as the government was then executing some important dredging work on the Clyde, directly between Helensburgh and Greenock – work that was being carried out in novel conditions using electric machines. Thus, once installed in the house, he would be able to watch the machines in use and calculate their usefulness and efficiency.

The Melville brothers could not but acknowledge how favourable this coincidence was to their plans. Whenever he was unoccupied, the young scientist would be able to follow the various phases of this very interesting work.

'But,' asked Aristobulus Ursiclos, 'you will no doubt have thought up some pretext for coming here, because Miss Campbell is undoubtedly not expecting to meet me in Oban?'

'Of course,' replied brother Sib, 'and this pretext was provided by Miss Campbell herself.'

'Ah', said the young scholar, 'and what is it?'

'It is a question of observing a physical phenomenon, which appears in certain conditions that do not arise in Helensburgh.'

'Indeed!' replied Aristobulus Ursiclos, adjusting his glasses with his finger. 'Gentlemen, this goes to prove that some natural affinity exists between Miss Campbell and myself! May I know

Oban

what the phenomenon is which cannot be studied in Helensburgh?'

'It is merely the Green Ray,' replied brother Sam.

'The Green Ray?' said Aristobulus Ursiclos, a little surprised. 'I have never heard of it! Dare I ask what this Green Ray is?'

The Melville brothers explained the nature of the phenomenon that the *Morning Post* had recently brought to the attention of its readers to the best of their ability.

'Bah!' said Aristobulus Ursiclos. 'It is only a mere curiosity of no great interest that falls under the somewhat childish category of amusing physics!'

'Miss Campbell is only a young girl,' brother Sib replied, 'and she seems to attach a great deal of importance, no doubt exaggerated, to this phenomenon...'

'She has said that she doesn't want to get married before she has seen it,' added brother Sam.

'Well, gentlemen,' replied Aristobulus Ursiclos, 'we will show her her Green Ray then!'

Then they all three, following the little path that ran through the fields next to the shore, made their way back towards the Caledonian Hotel.

Aristobulus Ursiclos did not lose this opportunity of pointing out to the Melville brothers how much women's minds delight in frivolity, and he gave a broad outline of all that would need to be done to raise the level of their neglected education. Not that he thought that their brains, which have a lesser supply of cerebral matter than those of men, and are very different in the arrangement of their lobes, would ever be able to arrive at the intelligence needed for lofty conjecture! But without going as far as that, perhaps it would be possible to modify them by special training, although, ever since there had been women in the world, never had one distinguished herself through one of those discoveries that have rendered illustrious the Aristotles, the Euclids, the Harveys, the Hahnemanns, the Pascals, the Newtons, the Laplaces, the Aragos, the Humphrey Davys, the Edisons, the Pasteurs and so on. He then launched into an explanation of various physical phenomena, and discoursed *de omni re scibili* without any further mention of Miss Campbell.

The Melville brothers listened to him faithfully – and all the more willingly as they would have been incapable of squeezing a single word into this monologue without paragraphs, which Aristobulus Ursiclos punctuated with imperious and educational hems and h'ms!

In this manner, they came to within a hundred paces of the Caledonian Hotel, and stopped there for a moment to take leave of one another.

A young girl was just then at the window of her room. She seemed very busy, even disconcerted. She looked forward, to the left, to the right, and appeared to be looking for a horizon that she could not see.

All of a sudden Miss Campbell – for it was she – noticed her uncles. The window was closed sharply straight away, and some moments later the young girl arrived on the shore, her arms half folded, her face severe and her expression full of reproach.

The Melville brothers looked at one another. Who was Helena angry with? Was it the presence of Aristobulus Ursiclos that was causing these symptoms of abnormal overexcitement?

In the meantime the young scholar had stepped forward and greeted Miss Campbell mechanically.

'Mr Aristobulus Ursiclos…' said brother Sam, introducing him ceremoniously.

'Who, by the greatest of coincidences, happens to be in Oban…!' added brother Sib.

'Ah! Mr Ursiclos?'

And Miss Campbell gave him the slightest of nods.

Then she turned towards the Melville brothers, who were somewhat ill-at-ease and hardly knew which way to look.

'Uncles?' she said severely.

'Dear Helena', the two uncles replied in the same worried tone of voice.

'Are we really in Oban?' she asked.

'In Oban? Of course.'

'And what brings you here, gentlemen?'

'On the Hebridean coast?'

'Most certainly.'

'Very well, then we won't be here in an hour's time!'

'In an hour's time?'

'Did I not ask you for a marine horizon?'

'Without a doubt, dear girl...'

'Would you be so good as to show me where it is?'

The Melville brothers looked around in astonishment.

Before them, both to the south-west and to the north-west, there appeared not a single interval between the islands out in the open sea, where the sky and the water merged together. Seil, Kerrera and Lismore formed a kind of continuous barrier from one piece of land to the next. They had to confess that the horizon that had been demanded and promised was absent from the landscape of Oban.

The two brothers had not even noticed this during their walk along the shore. They thus gave way to the following very Scottish interjections, which expressed real disappointment mixed with some ill-humour:

'Pooh!' said one.

'Pshaw!' said the other.

8

A Cloud on the Horizon

AN EXPLANATION HAD become necessary, but as it had nothing to do with Aristobulus Ursiclos, Miss Campbell took her leave of him coldly and returned to the Caledonian Hotel.

Aristobulus Ursiclos had taken his leave of the young girl equally coolly. Evidently offended at having been weighed against a ray, whatever its colour, he continued along the path on the shore, talking to himself in the most fitting terms.

Brother Sam and brother Sib felt uneasy, and so, once they were back in their private sitting room, they waited sheepishly for Miss Campbell to address them.

The discussion was short but to the point. They had come to Oban for a view of a marine horizon, and there wasn't one to be seen, or at least there was so little of one that it wasn't worth speaking of.

The two uncles could only argue that they had acted in good faith. They didn't know Oban! Who would have imagined that the sea, the real sea, was not there, since the bathers flocked to it! It was perhaps the only point on the coast where, thanks to these tiresome Hebridean islands, the circular line of water was not outlined against the sky!

'Well,' said Miss Campbell, in a tone that she tried to make as severe as possible, 'we must choose some place other than Oban, even though this means having to sacrifice the advantage of meeting Mr Aristobulus Ursiclos!'

The Melville brothers lowered their heads instinctively and made no reply to this direct shot.

'We will make our preparations and leave this very day,' said Miss Campbell.

'We'll leave!' replied the two uncles, who were only able to make amends for their mistake through an act of passive obedience.

And immediately the names echoed as usual:

'Bet!'

'Beth!'

'Bess!'

'Betsy!'

'Betty!'

Dame Bess arrived, followed by Partridge. They were both informed of the decision at once, and, knowing that their young mistress always had the final say, they did not enquire as to the motive of this hurried departure.

But they had reckoned without Mr MacFyne, the owner of the Caledonian Hotel.

You would know these estimable industrialists ill, even in hospitable Scotland, if you thought them capable of allowing a family of three masters and two servants to leave without having done everything possible to retain them. This is what happened on this occasion.

When he had been informed of this grave matter, Mr MacFyne declared that everything might be arranged to the satisfaction of all, not to mention his own particular satisfaction in being able to keep such distinguished travellers for as long as possible.

What did Miss Campbell want and, in consequence, what did Mr Sib and Mr Sam Melville desire? An open view of the sea with an extensive horizon? Nothing could be easier, since it was only a question of observing that horizon at sunset. They were unable to see it from the shore at Oban? True! Would it suffice to go and take up position on the isle of Kerrera? No. The large island of Mull would only allow a small portion of the Atlantic to be seen in the south-west. But further down the coast was the isle of Seil, which is connected to the mainland by a bridge at its northern tip.

There, there was nothing to impede their view to the west over two fifths of the compass.

Now it was a drive of only four to five miles to this island, no more, and, when the weather was favourable, an excellent carriage and good horses would be able to conduct Miss Campbell and her party there in an hour and a half.

In support of his statement, the eloquent hotel-keeper pointed to the large map hanging in the vestibule of the hotel. Miss Campbell was thus able to see that Mr MacFyne was not merely trying to be impressive. Indeed, off the isle of Seil was a large area, comprising a third of that horizon over which the sun sets during the weeks that precede and follow the equinox.

The matter was thus arranged to the extreme satisfaction of Mr MacFyne and to the Melville brothers' great convenience. Miss Campbell generously granted them her pardon, and made no more disagreeable allusions to the presence of Aristobulus Ursiclos.

'But,' said brother Sam, 'it is at least odd that there is no marine horizon to be found at Oban!'

'Nature is very strange!' replied brother Sib.

Aristobulus Ursiclos was no doubt very happy when he learnt that Miss Campbell was no longer going to look elsewhere for a more favourable location for her meteorological observations, but he was so absorbed in his lofty problems that he forgot to express his satisfaction.

The capricious young girl was probably grateful to him for his reserve, because, although she remained indifferent to him, she greeted him less coldly than on their first meeting.

In the meantime the state of the atmosphere had changed slightly. Although the weather remained fine, a few clouds, which dispelled the heat of midday, meant the horizon was cloudy at sunrise and sunset. There was thus no point in going to find an observation point on the island of Seil. It would have been a waste of effort; they had to remain patient.

During these long days, Miss Campbell, leaving her uncles to grapple with the fiancé of their choice, would wander along the shores of the bay, sometimes accompanied by dame Bess but more often alone. She was happy to escape the men and women of leisure who make up the fluctuating population of seaside towns, which is just about the same everywhere. It consists of families whose only occupation is to watch the sea going in and coming out, while small boys and girls roll about on the wet sand with a very British freedom of attitude; of grave and phlegmatic gentlemen, in bathing suits that are often very rudimentary, whose most important task in life is to immerse themselves in the salty water for six minutes; of highly respectable ladies and gentlemen, stiff and motionless on green benches with red cushions, and leafing through a few pages of those hardback books with dense text, which are garish and are overused somewhat in English editions; of a few passing tourists with lorgnettes slung over their shoulders, deerstalkers on their heads, long gaiters on their legs and umbrellas under their arms, who arrived yesterday and will leave again tomorrow. Then, in the midst of this crowd, are industrialists, whose business is essentially itinerant and portable; electricians, who, for two pence, sell that mysterious power to anyone who wants to satisfy their whim; artists, with piano organs that are mounted on wheels and which combine the distorted motifs of French tunes with Scottish ones; outdoor photographers who hand over snapshots by the dozen to families grouped for the occasion; merchants in black frockcoats, merchants in flowery hats, pushing their small carts on which is spread out the finest fruit in the world; and finally minstrels, whose grimacing faces are altered under the polish that covers them, acting out popular scenes with various fancy dresses and singing those local laments with countless verses, in the midst of a circle of children who solemnly join in the chorus together.

For Miss Campbell, this life at a seaside town had no further secrets, nor did it have any charm. She preferred to get away from this coming and going of passers-by, who seem as unfamiliar to each other as if they came from all four corners of Europe.

So, when her uncles became worried by her absence and wanted to find her, they had to go looking at the edge of the shore at some headland jutting out in the bay.

There Miss Campbell would be seated, like the pensive Minna

While small boys and girls roll about on the sand...

in *The Pirate,* her elbow on the projecting part of a rock, her head leaning on one hand, whilst the other picked at the berries of that fennel type plant that grows between the stones. Her absent gaze wandered from a stack, whose rocky summit rose steeply upwards, to some obscure cavern, one of those 'helyers' as they are called in Scotland, howling with the ebb of the sea.

Far away were rows of cormorants, sitting motionless like hieratic beasts. Her eyes followed them in the distance when their tranquillity was disturbed and they flew off, skimming the crests of the small waves that made up the surf with their wings.

What was the young girl thinking about? Aristobulus Ursiclos would undoubtedly have had the impertinence, and her uncles the naivety, to think that she was thinking of him: they would have been wrong.

In her mind, Miss Campbell was revisiting the scenes at Corryvreckan. She saw the rowing boat in distress, the manoeuvres of the *Glengarry* as it ventured into the middle of the channel. Deep in her heart she once again experienced that emotion that had gripped her so tightly when the imprudent pair had disappeared into the centre of the eddy! Then the rescue, the rope thrown at an opportune moment, the elegant young man appearing on the bridge, calm, smiling, less emotional than she was, and saluting the passengers of the steamer.

Here were the beginnings of a novel for any romantic mind, but it seemed that the novel would be confined to this first chapter. The book, which had been begun, had closed again abruptly in Miss Campbell's hands. At what page would she ever be able to open it again, since 'her hero', like some Wodan from Gaelic epics, had not reappeared?

But had she at least looked for him in the midst of this crowd of indifferent persons, who haunted the beaches of Oban? Perhaps. Had she met him? No. He would no doubt have been unable to recognise her. Why would he have noticed her on board the *Glengarry*? Why would he have come to her? How could he have guessed that he owed his rescue in part to her? And yet it was she who had been the first to notice the boat in distress; she who had been the first to beg the captain to go to the rescue! And, in fact, it had perhaps that evening cost her the sight of the Green Ray! It was to be feared so at least.

During the three days that followed the Melville family's arrival in Oban, the sky would have driven the astronomers in the observatories of Edinburgh and Greenwich to despair. It seemed to be blanketed in a sort of haze that was more of a disappointment than clouds would have been. The most powerful models of telescopes, and even the reflectors in Cambridge and in Parsonstown, would have been unable to pierce it. Only the sun would have possessed enough power to penetrate it with its rays, but, at sunset, the marine horizon became indistinct in light mists that turned the west the most splendid shades of crimson. It was thus not possible for the green arrow to reach the eyes of an observer.

In her daydream Miss Campbell, carried away by her somewhat fantastical imagination, mixed up the wreck from the Gulf of Corryvreckan and the Green Ray in the same thought. Certain it was that neither the one nor the other appeared. If the haze obscured the latter, the other remained incognito.

The Melville brothers, when they took it into their heads to urge their niece to be patient, were in no position to do so. Miss Campbell did not hesitate to render them responsible for the atmospheric disturbances. They thus placed the blame on the excellent aneroid barometer, which they had taken care to bring with them from Helensburgh and whose needle persistently refused to rise. In all honesty, they would have given up their snuff box to obtain a cloudless sky when the radiant star was setting!

As for the scholar Aristobulus Ursiclos, one day, when speaking of the haze that covered the horizon, he had the tactlessness to pronounce its formation quite natural. From there it was only a small step to the start of a short physics lesson, and this in the presence of Miss Campbell. He spoke of clouds in general, of their downward movement, which brings them to the horizon as the temperature drops, of haze reduced to a vesicular state, of the scientific classification of clouds as nimbus, stratus, cumulus and cirrus! Needless to say what he received for his erudition. And this was so marked that the Melville brothers didn't know what to do during this inopportune discourse!

Yes! Miss Campbell pointedly 'cut' the young scholar, to use the expression of modern dandyism. First of all she affected to look in a completely different direction so as not to listen to him, then she obstinately raised her eyes towards Dunolly Castle so as to appear not to notice him, and finally she looked at the tips of her sand shoes, which is the most marked form of indifference, the greatest proof of disdain that a Scotswoman can show, and is as much for what her interlocutor is saying as for the person himself.

Aristobulus Ursiclos, who neither saw nor heard anything other than himself, who never spoke for anyone other than himself, didn't notice, or seemed not to notice.

In this manner the 3, 4, 5 and 6 of August passed away, but, during that last day, to the great joy of the Melville brothers, the barometer rose several lines above variable.

The following day thus got off to the most auspicious start. At ten o'clock in the morning the sun was shining brilliantly, and the azure sky above the sea was perfectly clear.

Miss Campbell could not let this opportunity pass. A carriage was always kept ready for her in the stables of the Caledonian Hotel. The moment to use it was now or never.

Thus, at five o'clock in the evening, Miss Campbell and the Melville brothers took their seats in the carriage, which was driven by a coachman who was skilful at manoeuvring the four-in-hand. Partridge climbed up onto the back seat, and the four horses, caressed by the lash of the long whip, set off on the road from Oban to Clachan.

Aristobulus Ursiclos, to his great regret, though not to that of Miss Campbell, was busy with some important scientific paper and thus was not able to be of the party.

The excursion was charming throughout. The carriage followed the coastal road along the strait that separates the isle of Kerrera from the Scottish mainland. This island, of volcanic origin, was very picturesque, but it had one fault in Miss Campbell's eyes; it hid the marine horizon from her. However, as there were only four and a half miles to traverse in these circumstances, she consented to admire its harmonious profile, which was outlined against a background of light, with the ruins of the Danish castle crowning its southern tip.

'It used to be the residence of the MacDougals of Lorn', observed brother Sam.

'And for our family', added brother Sib, 'this castle is of historical interest, as it was destroyed by the Campbells who set fire to it after massacring all its inhabitants mercilessly!'

This heroic deed appeared to gain the particular approbation of Partridge, who clapped his hands softly in honour of the clan.

When they had passed the isle of Kerrera, the carriage took a straight and slightly uneven road, which led to the village of Clachan. There it crossed that artificial isthmus which, in the form of a bridge, straddles the small channel and unites the isle of Seil and the mainland. Half an hour later, having left the carriage at the foot of a ravine, the travellers climbed the somewhat steep slope of a hill and sat down on the very edge of the rocks beside the coast.

This time nothing could possibly obstruct their view to the west, neither the small island of Easdale, nor that of Insh, both of which lay close to Seil. Between Ardalanish Point on the Isle of Mull, one of the largest of the Hebridean islands, to the north-east and the island of Colonsay to the south-west, was a large expanse of sea, upon which the fire of the solar disc would soon drown.

Miss Campbell, deep in thought, was slightly in front. Only a few birds of prey, eagles or hawks, brought life to this solitude, hovering above their lairs, which were like shell holes in rocky walls.

Astronomically, at this time of year and at this latitude, the sun should set at seven fifty-four, exactly in the direction of Ardalanish Point.

But some weeks later it would have been impossible to see it disappear beneath the sea, because the island of Colonsay would have concealed it from view.

So this evening, both time and place had been well chosen for the observation of the phenomenon.

At that moment the sun was making its way towards the perfectly cloudless horizon along an oblique trajectory.

Their eyes found it difficult to stand the brilliance of the ardent red disk, which the water reflected in a long train of light.

However, neither Miss Campbell nor her uncles would have consented to close their eyes – no, not even for an instant!

But, before the star had touched the horizon with its lower edge, Miss Campbell gave a cry of disappointment!

A small cloud had just appeared, as slender as an arrow and as long as the pennant of a warship. It cut the disk into two uneven parts, and seemed to sink with it down to sea level.

It seemed as though the slightest breeze would have sufficed to drive it away and to disperse it! But the breeze didn't come!

And when the sun was reduced to a tiny arc, it was this thin haze that covered the line separating the sky and the water.

The Green Ray, lost in this little cloud, was hidden from the eyes of the observers.

9

The Words of Dame Bess

THE DRIVE BACK TO Oban took place in silence. Miss Campbell didn't speak; the Melville brothers didn't dare to speak. And yet it was not their fault if this untimely haze had appeared at precisely the moment when it would absorb the sun's last ray. After all, there was no need to despair. The good weather ought to last for more than six weeks yet. If, during the entire duration of autumn, no fine evening should appear, bringing with it a cloudless horizon, they really would have been dogged by ill luck!

However, a splendid evening had been lost, and the barometer did not seem to promise another similar – at least not soon. Indeed, during the night the aneroid barometer's capricious needle fell slightly towards variable. But what was still fine weather for everyone else could not satisfy Miss Campbell.

The next day, the 8 August, the sun's rays were veiled by a warm haze. This time, the midday breeze was not strong enough to disperse it. Towards evening the sky turned a vivid shade of crimson. The array of colours, from chrome-yellow to a sombre ultramarine, made the horizon into a brilliant artist's pallet. Under the fluffy veil of small clouds, the sunset tinted the background of the coast with all the rays in the spectrum, except the one that the fanciful and superstitious Miss Campbell was anxious to see.

And it was the same the following day, and then the day after that. Thus the coach remained in the hotel's shed. What was the use of going out to make an observation that the state of the sky rendered impossible? The heights of the isle of Seil could be no more favoured than the beaches of Oban, and it was better not to head for more disappointment.

Without being in a worse mood than might have been expected, Miss Campbell contented herself with retiring to her room when evening came, refusing to have anything to do with this unaccomodating sun. There, whilst resting after her long walks, she would daydream. Of what? Of the legend that is connected with the Green Ray? Was it still necessary for her to see it in order to see clearly into her heart? Perhaps not into her own, but what about into that of others?

That day, accompanied by dame Bess, Helena had carried her disappointment to Dunolly Castle. At this spot, from the foot of an old wall, which was covered with thick, vertical strands of ivy, nothing could have been more lovely than the panorama formed by the indentation of the bay of Oban, the wild appearance of Kerrera, the isles scattered in the Hebridean sea and the large Isle of Mull, whose rocky western coast receives the first onslaught from the storms arriving from the western Atlantic.

And so Miss Campbell gazed upon the magnificent view spread out before her eyes, but did she see it? Or did some memory persist in distracting her? It can at least be said that it was not the image of Aristobulus Ursiclos. In truth, the young pedant's presence would have been unfortunate, given the opinions that dame Bess expressed so frankly about him that day.

'I don't like him!' she repeated. 'No! I don't like him! He only thinks of himself! What sort of figure would he cut in Helensburgh? He is of the 'MacEgoist' clan or I'm very much mistaken! How could my masters ever have thought of him becoming their nephew? Partridge can't bear him anymore than I can, and Partridge is no fool! Come now Miss Campbell, do you like him?'

'Of whom are you speaking?' asked the young girl, who had not heard anything that dame Bess had said.

'Of someone who you cannot consider... were it only for the honour of the clan!'

'And who, then, do you think I cannot consider?'

'Mr Aristobulus Ursiclos of course, who had better go looking

Miss Campbell gazed upon the magnificent view...

on the other side of the Tweed, as if a Campbell would ever go after an Ursiclos!'

Dame Bess did not usually mince her words, but she had to be singularly aroused to contradict her masters – though it is true it was for the benefit of her young mistress! Moreover, she was aware that Helena showed little more than indifference for this suitor. To tell the truth, she could hardly have imagined that this indifference was coupled with a keener sentiment felt for another.

However, perhaps dame Bess did begin to have her suspicions when Miss Campbell asked her if she had seen the young man to whom the *Glengarry* had so fortunately offered help and assistance in Oban.

'No, Miss Campbell', dame Bess replied, 'he must have left straight away, though Partridge thinks he saw him...'

'When?'

'Yesterday on the Dalmally road. He was returning with a bag on his back, like a travelling artist! Oh, what an imprudent young man he is! To allow himself to be carried into the Gulf of Corryvreckan in such a way, it augurs badly for the future! He won't always find a boat ready to come to his aid, something bad will happen to him!'

'Do you think so, Bess? He might have been imprudent, but he at least showed that he had courage, and in the midst of his peril his self-possession doesn't seem to have left him for a moment!'

'Quite possibly, but what is certain, Miss Campbell,' resumed dame Bess, 'is that that young man didn't know that he perhaps owed his rescue to you, or he would at least have come to thank you the day after arriving in Oban ...'

'To thank me?' replied Miss Campbell. 'Why? I only did for him what I would have done for anyone else and, trust me, what anyone else would have done in my place!'

'Would you recognise him?' asked dame Bess, looking at the young girl.

'Yes,' replied Miss Campbell frankly, 'and I confess that his character, the calm courage that he showed when he appeared on the bridge, as though he hadn't just escaped death, and the affectionate words he spoke to his old companion whilst he pressed him to his chest, made a great impression on me!'

'Well,' replied the worthy woman, 'I can hardly say what he's like, but, at any rate, it isn't Mr Aristobulus Ursiclos!'

Miss Campbell smiled without saying a word, rose and then stood motionless for a moment, casting one last look at the distant heights of the Isle of Mull. Then, followed by dame Bess, she descended the arid path that led to the Oban road.

That evening the sun set in a kind of luminous dust, as light as glittery tulle, and its last ray was absorbed once again in the evening mists.

Miss Campbell thus returned to the hotel, did little justice to the dinner that her uncles had ordered for her, and, after a short walk on the shore, returned to her room.

10

A Game of Croquet

IT MUST BE confessed that the Melville brothers were beginning to count the days as they passed, though they were not yet at the stage of counting hours. Things were not going as they would have wanted. Their niece's visible ennui and her need to be alone, as well as the poor welcome she gave to the scholar Aristobulus Ursiclos, and with which the latter was perhaps less preoccupied than they themselves were, all that did not render their stay in Oban pleasant. They were at a loss to know how to break this monotony. They watched in vain for the slightest atmospheric change. They told themselves that, once her desire had been satisfied, Miss Campbell would undoubtedly become more accommodating – at least to them.

The fact was, for the last two days, Helena had become even more preoccupied than before, and had forgotten to give them the morning kiss that put them in good humour for the rest of the day.

Meanwhile, the barometer, impervious to the remonstrations of the two uncles, did not show any inclination to predict a change in the weather in the near future. Though they took care to give it a little sharp tap ten times a day so as to cause the needle to waver, it did not rise a single line. Oh, those barometers!

All of a sudden the Melville brothers had an idea. On the afternoon of the 11 August, they thought of proposing a croquet game to Miss Campbell, so as to distract her if possible, and, even though Aristobulus Ursiclos had to be of the party, Helena did not refuse, as she knew that it would give them pleasure.

The ball, deftly struck…

It must be said that brother Sam and brother Sib prided them-selves on being first-class players of this game, which is so favoured in the United Kingdom. It is only, as is well-known, the ancient game of 'pall mall', very successfully adapted to the taste of young ladies.

Now in Oban there were several areas laid out for the playing of croquet. If, in the majority of seaside towns, people are content with a lawn or strand that is more or less level, it proves less the demand of the players and more their indifference or lack of zeal for this noble pastime. Here were real croquet grounds, made not of sand but of grass, as is proper, which were watered every evening with sprinklers, rolled every morning with a special machine, and which were as soft as steamrollered velvet. Small squares of stone showing on the surface of the ground were destined for the pegs and hoops. In addition, a ditch, several inches deep, divided the grounds and gave them the twelve hundred square feet necessary to the players.

How many times the Melville brothers had watched the move-ments of young men and women on these elite grounds with envy! So what satisfaction they felt when Miss Campbell accepted their invitation. They would be able to amuse her whilst indulging in their favourite game, and all in the midst of spectators, for there would be plenty here, as in Helensburgh! How vain they were!

Aristobulus Ursiclos, duly informed, had agreed to break off from his work, and was at the battleground at the appointed hour. He laid claim to being as good at croquet in theory as he was in practice, and to playing it as a scholar, a geometrician, a physicist and a mathematician; in short, by the rule of A + B as was appro-priate to a head full of x's.

Miss Campbell was not altogether pleased at having to have this young pedant as a partner. But how could it be otherwise? Would she give her uncles the pain of separating them in the fight, of making them face one another, they who were so united in thought and heart, in body and mind, they who only ever played together! No! She would not have wanted to!

'Miss Campbell,' Aristobulus Ursiclos said to her firstly, 'I am

93

most happy to be your second, and if you will allow me, I will explain the factors determining the strokes to you...'

'Mr Ursiclos,' replied Helena taking him to one side, 'we have to let my uncles win.'

'Win?'

'Yes, without seeming to do so.'

'But Miss Campbell...'

'They would be so unhappy if they lost...'

'Nevertheless...' replied Aristobulus Ursiclos, 'I'm very sorry but I know the game of croquet geometrically, and I can be proud of it! I have calculated the combination of lines and the value of curves, and I think I can lay claim to...'

'I can only lay claim,' replied Miss Campbell, 'to being agreeable to my adversaries. Anyway, they are very good at croquet, I warn you, and I don't think that your science will be able to beat their skill.'

'We shall see,' murmured Aristobulus Ursiclos. No consideration could ever have determined him to allow himself to be beaten voluntarily – not even that of pleasing Miss Campbell.

Meanwhile the box containing the pegs, markers, hoops, balls and mallets had been brought by the boy on duty at the croquet ground.

The hoops, nine in all, were set out in a diamond shape on the small slabs, and the two pegs stood at each end of the diamond's large axis.

'Let's draw lots!' said brother Sam.

The markers were placed in a hat. Each player took one at random.

Fate delivered the following colours and order to the game: a blue mallet and ball to brother Sam, a red mallet and ball to Ursiclos, a yellow mallet and ball to brother Sib and a green mallet and ball to Miss Campbell.

'And I'm waiting for a ray of the same colour,' she said, 'it's a good sign!'

Brother Sam was to begin, and he did so after taking a good pinch of snuff with his partner.

You should have seen him, his body neither too straight nor

Miss Campbell was playing very well...

too bent, his head half-turned to enable him to hit the ball at exactly the right spot, his hands placed one next to the other on the handle of the mallet, the left below, the right above, his legs steady, his knees slightly bent to counterbalance the force of the blow, his left foot next to the ball, his right foot a little behind! A typical example of an accomplished croquet-playing gentleman!

Brother Sam then raised his mallet with a gentle semi-circular movement, and struck the ball that had been placed eighteen inches from the starting peg. He didn't need to make use of the right he had to recommence this initial operation three times. Indeed the ball, deftly struck, passed through the first hoop and then through the second. Another strike and it cleared the third, and it was only when entering the fourth that it struck the iron side and stopped.

It was a magnificent start, and a very flattering murmur ran through the spectators who were standing on the other side of the small ditch surrounding the grassy area.

It was now Aristobulus Ursiclos' turn. He was less fortunate. Whether through bad play or bad luck, he had to make three attempts to get his ball through the first hoop, and then it missed the second.

'It is very probable,' he observed to Miss Campbell, 'that the calibre of this ball is not quite perfect, in which case its centre of gravity, placed eccentrically, will cause it to veer off course.'

'Your turn, uncle Sib,' said Miss Campbell, taking no notice of this scientific explanation.

Brother Sib was worthy of brother Sam. His ball passed through two hoops and stopped near to Aristobulus Ursiclos' ball, which he made use of to pass through the third after roqueting it, which means striking it from a distance. He then roqueted the young scientist once again, whose entire countenance seemed to say: 'we can do better than that!' Finally, having brought the two balls into contact with one another, he placed his foot on his own, struck it vigorously with his mallet and croqueted his opponent's ball. In other words, a ricochet effect sent it flying sixty paces away beyond the ditch serving as a boundary.

Aristobulus Ursiclos was obliged to run after his ball, but he did so in a most composed manner, like a man deep in thought, and he waited in the attitude of a general who is meditating his master stroke.

Miss Campbell took her green ball in turn and deftly passed it through the first two hoops.

The game continued in a manner that was very much to the advantage of the Melville brothers, who had great fun roqueting and croqueting their opponents' balls. What a massacre! They communicated using small signs and understood each other at a glance, without even needing to speak, and, finally, got a long way ahead to the great satisfaction of their niece, but to the great displeasure of Aristobulus Ursiclos.

In the meantime Miss Campbell, seeing that she was a sufficient distance behind five minutes after the start of the game, began to play more seriously, and showed much more aptitude than her partner, who, nonetheless, did not spare her his scientific advice.

'The angle of reflection', he said to her, 'is equal to the angle of incidence, which should indicate to you the direction that the balls will take after they are hit. It is thus necessary to take advantage of…'

'You take advantage of it then', replied Miss Campbell. 'Here I am, sir, three hoops ahead of you!'

And indeed Aristobulus Ursiclos lagged sadly behind. He had already attempted to pass through the double hoop in the centre ten times without success. He thus began to complain of it, and, after having it straightened up and the gap altered, tried his luck once more.

Fortune did not favour him. His ball struck the iron frame every time without managing to pass through it.

In fact Miss Campbell would have been within her rights to have complained of her partner. She herself was playing very well and deserved the compliments that her uncles lavished on her. Nothing could have been more charming than to watch her complete dedication to this game, which is so well designed for developing physical grace: her right foot half raised so as to hold her ball when it croqueted another, her arms coquettishly rounded as she moved her mallet through half a circle, the animation of her

'Usually you warn people before beginning a bombardment!'

pretty face, bent slightly towards the ground, and the delightful sway of her waist were a delight to behold! And yet Aristobulus Ursiclos saw nothing of it.

It must be owned that the young scholar was enraged. In fact, the Melville brothers had now got such a lead that it would be difficult to catch them. And yet the uncertainties of the game of croquet are so unexpected that victory is never to be despaired of.

The game was thus continuing in these unequal conditions when an incident occurred.

Aristobulus Ursiclos finally had the chance to roquet brother Sam's ball, which had just passed through the central hoop again, before which he himself was obstinately held. Greatly vexed, though trying hard to remain calm in the eyes of the spectators, he determined to play a master-stroke, and to give his adversary a taste of his own medicine, by sending him beyond the boundary of the playing area. He thus placed his ball close to brother Sam's, ensured that it was touching by packing down the grass with the greatest of care, placed his left foot on it, and, moving his mallet through an almost complete circle, so as to give the blow more force, he whirled it round quickly.

What a cry arose from him! It was a howl of pain! The mallet had been but poorly directed and had struck the clumsy player's foot instead of his ball, and there he was hopping around on one leg and uttering groans, which was undoubtedly very natural but somewhat ridiculous.

The Melville brothers ran to him. Fortunately the leather of his boot had deadened the force of the blow, and the bruise was not serious. But Aristobulus Ursiclos thought proper to explain his misadventure as follows: 'The radius traced by my mallet,' he said pompously though not without a grimace, 'followed a circle concentric to that which should have tangentially skimmed the ground, because I kept the radius a little too short. Hence this blow...'

'Well sir, shall we stop the game?' asked Miss Campbell.

'Stop the game!' cried Aristobulus Ursiclos. 'Confess that we are beaten? Never! If you take the formulas used for the calculation of probability, you will still find...'

'So be it! Let's continue!' replied Miss Campbell.

But all the formulas used for the calculation of probability would have given very little chance to the opponents of the two uncles. Brother Sam was already a 'rover'; in other words, his ball having gone through all the hoops, he had struck the finishing peg and all he had to do now was to come to his partner's aid by croqueting or roqueting any ball that he wished.

In fact, a few more strokes decided the game and the Melville brothers triumphed, though modestly as becomes experts. As for Aristobulus Ursiclos, despite his pretensions, he had not even managed to get through the central hoop.

Undoubtedly Miss Campbell wanted to appear more vexed than she really was, and, with a vigorous blow of her mallet, she struck her ball with little regard to direction.

The ball soared out of the boundary marked by the little ditch in the direction of the sea, bounced up on a pebble and, as Aristobulus Ursiclos would have said, aided by its weight multiplied by the square of its velocity, flew past the edge of the shore.

It was an unlucky stroke!

A young artist was sitting there in front of his easel, making a sketch of the sea as far as the southern tip of Oban's harbour. The ball struck the canvas full on, smeared all the colours in the pallet, which it brushed against when passing, over its green surface, and knocked the easel over.

The painter calmly turned around and said: 'Usually you warn people before beginning a bombardment. We're not safe here!'

Miss Campbell, sensing that the accident would happen before it had taken place, had run to the shore: 'Oh, sir!' she said to the young artist, 'please forgive my clumsiness!'

The man stood up and bowed smilingly to the embarrassed young girl, who had just made her apologies.

It was the victim of the Corryvreckan shipwreck!

11

Oliver Sinclair

OLIVER SINCLAIR WAS a 'bonnie lad', to employ the expression formerly in common use in Scotland when speaking of gallant, quick
and alert young men, but if this expression suited him in a moral
sense, it must be said that it suited him no less in a physical one.

He was the last offshoot of a respectable Edinburgh family; this
young Athenian from the Athens of the North was the son of a
former councillor of the capital of Midlothian. He had lost his
father and mother and had been brought up by his uncle, one of the
four bailiffs of the municipal administration. He had studied hard at
the university, then, at the age of twenty, with a small fortune
assuring him independence at least and curious to see the world,
he had visited the principal states in Europe, India and America,
and the famous *Edinburgh Review* had, on occasion, published
his travel notes. He was a distinguished painter, who could have
sold his work at a high price had he wanted to, and a poet when
he felt like it – and who is not at an age when existence as a whole
smiles at you? He had a warm heart and an artistic nature; he was
made to please and did so without affectation or smugness.

It is easy to get married in the capital of old Caledonia. In fact,
the sexes are in very unequal proportion there, and, in terms of
number, the weaker sex prevails considerably over the stronger. Thus
an educated, amiable, respectable young man, with a handsome
figure, cannot fail to find there more than one heiress who is to
his liking.

And yet Oliver Sinclair, at twenty-six years of age, did not yet
seem to have felt the need to live a married life. Did then the path

through life appear to him too narrow to walk side by side? Undoubtedly the answer is no. It is more likely that he felt it was better to walk alone, to take short cuts and to run when he so wished, particularly with his tastes for art and travel.

Nevertheless, Oliver Sinclair was of the sort to inspire more than friendship in any young, fair daughter of Scotland. His elegant figure, his open physiognomy, his frank air, his manly countenance with its strong features and soft eyes, the grace and ease with which he moved, the refinement of his manners, his easy and witty conversation, and his casual gait were all designed to charm. But he had very little suspicion of this, for he was not conceited, or else did not think about it, for he was not inclined to bind himself to another. Moreover, if he was the subject of flattering appraisal amongst the female clan of Auld Reeky, he was nonetheless liked by his youthful companions and his comrades at the university. He was one of those people 'who never turn their back on friend or foe', as the pleasant Gaelic saying goes.

And yet, that day when the attack took place, it must be acknowledged that he did have his back turned on Miss Campbell. Miss Campbell, it is true, was neither his enemy nor his friend. Thus, in that attitude, he had been unable to see the approach of ball that the young girl had struck so vigorously with her mallet. Hence the shell-like effect on his canvas and the toppling of all his painting paraphernalia.

Miss Campbell had recognised her Corryvreckan 'hero' at first glance, but the hero had not recognised the young passenger from the *Glengarry*. He had barely noticed Miss Campbell on board during the final part of the crossing from the isle of Scarba to Oban. Had he known what part she herself had played in his rescue, he would most certainly have thanked her more particularly, were it only out of politeness, but he was still unaware of it, and he would probably always remain so.

And indeed, that very day, Miss Campbell forbade, yes, absolutely forbade, both her uncles and dame Bess and Partridge from making any allusion in front of this young man to what had happened on board the *Glengarry* before the rescue.

Meanwhile, after the accident with the ball, the Melville brothers had rejoined their niece, more disconcerted than she herself were that possible, and they began to offer their personal apologies to the young painter, when the latter interrupted them: 'Miss, gentlemen, I beg you, there really is no need!'

'No, sir,' insisted brother Sib, 'we are truly sorry...'

'And if the calamity cannot be put right, as is to be feared...' added brother Sam.

'It was only an accident, it isn't a calamity!' replied the young man with a laugh. 'A daub, nothing more, to which this avenging ball did justice!'

Oliver Sinclair said this with so much good humour that the Melville brothers would willingly have shaken hands with him without further ceremony. In any case, they thought it right to introduce themselves, as gentlemen should.

'Mr Samuel Melville', said one.

'Mr Sebastian Melville', said the other.

'And their niece, Miss Campbell', added Helena, who thought it quite proper to introduce herself.

It was an invitation to the young man to state his name and particulars.

'Miss Campbell, gentlemen,' he said very seriously, 'I could reply that I am called after one of the pegs in your croquet game, since I was touched by the ball, but I am quite simply called Oliver Sinclair.'

'Mr Sinclair,' replied Miss Campbell, who didn't quite know what to make of this reply, 'once again, please accept my apologies...'

'And ours', added the Melville brothers.

'Miss Campbell,' resumed Oliver Sinclair, 'I repeat, it isn't worth thinking about. I was trying to obtain the effect of waves breaking, and it is highly likely that your ball, like the sponge of I know not which painter from the antiquity, which was thrown across his painting, will have produced the effect that my brush was trying in vain to create!'

It was said in such an amiable tone that Miss Campbell and the Melville brothers could not help smiling.

As for the canvas that Oliver Sinclair picked up, it was ruined and would have to be begun again.

It might as well be remarked that Aristobulus Ursiclos had not come across to participate in this exchange of apologies and polite remarks.

When the game had finished, the young scholar, very vexed at not having been able to make his theoretical knowledge agree with his practical aptitude, had left to return to his hotel. They were not to see him again for three or four days, as he was going to leave for the isle of Luing, one of the smallest of the Hebridean islands, situated to the south of the isle of Seil, for he wanted to study its rich slate quarries from a geological point of view.

They were thus not bothered by the explanatory interventions that he would have been sure to make in relation to the pressure on trajectories or other questions relating to the accident.

Oliver Sinclair soon learnt that he was not a complete stranger to the guests of the Caledonian Hotel, and he was informed of the incidents of the crossing.

'What!', he cried, 'Miss Campbell and you gentlemen were on board the *Glengarry*, which fished me out so opportunely?'

'Yes, Mr Sinclair.'

'And you really scared us,' added brother Sib, 'when, by the greatest of chances, we noticed your boat lost in the eddy of Corryvreckan!'

'By a lucky chance,' added brother Sam, 'and, very likely, without the intervention of...'

It is here that Miss Campbell gave him to understand by a small sign that she did not mean to be set up as a liberator. The role of Our Lady of Shipwrecks was not one that she meant to accept at any price.

'But Mr Sinclair', resumed brother Sam, 'how came the old fisherman who was with you to be so imprudent as to venture into the currents'

'He must have been well aware of their danger, since he is from this area?' added brother Sib.

'He should not be blamed, gentlemen', replied Oliver Sinclair. 'I was the imprudent one, I alone, and I thought for an instant

that I would have to reproach myself for the death of that coura-
geous man! But the colours were so wonderful on the surface of
the eddy, where the sea resembles an immense piece of guipure lace
thrown over a blue silk background! So, without worrying about
anything else, I set out in search of new shades of colour in the midst
of this foam, which was impregnated with light. I went closer and
closer! My old fisherman sensed the danger and remonstrated
with me, he wanted to return to the coast of Jura, but I barely listened to him, so much so that our boat was finally caught by a
current and then irresistibly dragged towards the gulf! We tried to
fight its lure! A heavy swell injured my companion, who was
unable to help me, and certainly, had the *Glengarry* not arrived,
without the captain's dedication and the humanity of the passengers, my companion and I would have passed into that legendary
state of being catalogued in the obituary list for Corryvreckan!'

Miss Campbell listened without saying a word, occasionally
raising her beautiful eyes to look at the young man, who did not
attempt to embarrass her by returning her gaze. She was unable to
prevent herself from smiling when he spoke of his hunt, or rather
of his fish, for marine hues. Was not she too in pursuit of similar
adventure, a little less perilous however, in her hunt for celestial
shades, in her hunt for the Green Ray?

And the Melville brothers were unable to refrain from men-
tioning it when speaking of the motive that had brought them to
Oban, that is to say the observation of a physical phenomenon,
whose nature they explained to the young painter.

'The Green Ray?' cried Oliver Sinclair.

'Have you already seen it, sir?' the young girl asked keenly,
'have you already seen it?

'No, Miss Campbell', replied Oliver Sinclair. 'I didn't even
know that there was such a thing as a Green Ray? Truly I didn't!
Well, I want to see it as well! The sun will not disappear beneath
the horizon again without having me for a witness! And, by St
Dunstan, I will paint again only with the green of its last ray!'

It was difficult to know whether Oliver Sinclair was speaking
slightly ironically, or whether he was allowing himself to be carried

away by the artist within him. However, Miss Campbell had a feeling that the young man was not joking.

'Mr Sinclair,' she resumed, 'the Green Ray is not my property! It shines for everyone! It loses none of its value by appearing to several interested people at once! So we can, if you wish, try to find it together.'

'I would be very happy to, Miss Campbell.'

'But lots of patience is required.'

'We will be patient...'

'And you must not be afraid of hurting your eyes', said brother Sam.

'The Green Ray is well worth that risk,' replied Oliver Sinclair, 'and I will not leave Oban without having seen it, I promise.'

'We have already been to the isle of Seil once to observe the ray', said Miss Campbell, 'but a little cloud appeared and veiled the horizon, just at the moment when the sun was setting.'

'How unfortunate!'

'Truly unfortunate, Mr Sinclair, for since that day the sky has never again been clear enough for us.'

'It will return, Miss Campbell! The summer has not yet spoken its last, and believe me, before the return of the bad weather, the sun will have favoured us with the Green Ray.'

'To tell you the truth, Mr Sinclair,' resumed Miss Campbell, 'we would certainly have seen it on the evening of the 2 August, over the horizon of the Gulf of Corryvreckan, had our attention not been distracted by a certain rescue...'

'What, Miss Campbell,' replied Oliver Sinclair, 'I was clumsy enough to distract your eyes at such a moment! My imprudence cost you the Green Ray! Well, it is I who owe you an apology, and I would like to express my regret for my inopportune intervention! It will not happen again!'

And they continued to speak of one thing or another whilst walking back to the Caledonian Hotel, where Oliver Sinclair had arrived the day before, after returning from an excursion to the environs of Dalmally. This young man, whose frank manners and infectious gaiety were not unpleasing to the two brothers – indeed far from it –, was then induced to speak of Edinburgh and his uncle, the bailiff Patrick Oldimer. It so happened that the Melville brothers had been connected with the bailiff, Oldimer, for several years. The two families had formerly been on sociable terms, which distance alone had interrupted. They thus found themselves perfectly acquainted, and Oliver Sinclair was invited to renew the family friendship with the Melvilles, and, as there was no reason why he should not pitch his artistic tent in Oban, he declared himself more than ever resolved to remain there, so as to participate in the search for the famous ray.

Miss Campbell and the Melville brothers thus met him frequently on the beaches of Oban in the days that followed. Together they observed whether the atmospheric conditions were likely to change. Ten times a day they checked the barometer, which showed some vague propensity to rise. And indeed, that amiable instrument rose above thirty inches and seven tenths on the morning of the 14 August.

With what delight Oliver Sinclair brought the good news to Miss Campbell that day! A sky pure as the eye of a madonna! A sky whose shades ranged from indigo to ultramarine! No hygrometric vapour anywhere! The prospect of a splendid evening and of a sunset that would have astonished the astronomers in an observatory!

'If we don't see our ray at sunset,' said Oliver Sinclair, 'it will be because we are blind!'

'Uncles', replied Miss Campbell, 'you do understand that it's this evening!'

It was thus agreed that they would leave for the isle of Seil before dinner. And that is exactly what they did at five o'clock.

The coach drove them along the picturesque Clachan road. Miss Campbell was radiant with happiness, Oliver Sinclair was beaming, and the Melville brothers were sharing in their radiance and rapture. You really could have said that they were taking the sun with them on the seat of their carriage, and that the four horses in the quick equipage were the hippogryphs from Apollo's chariot, and that he was the god of the hour!

Along the picturesque Clachan road...

When they arrived at the isle of Seil, the enthusiastic observers found themselves faced with a horizon whose lines were not distorted by any obstacle. They went and seated themselves at the end of a narrow headland, which separated two inlets of the coast and extended out a mile into the sea. Nothing could impede the view to the west of a quarter of the horizon.

'So we are finally going to see this capricious ray, which is so reluctant to alow itself to be seen!' said Oliver Sinclair.

'I believe so', replied brother Sam.

'I am sure of it', added brother Sib.

'And I hope so', replied Miss Campbell, looking at the empty sea and the clear sky.

In fact, everything seemed to suggest that the phenomenon would be revealed, in all its splendour, at sunset.

Already the radiant star, sinking in an oblique line, was only a few degrees above the horizon. Its red disk stained the background of the sky a uniform colour, and threw a long dazzling train on the sleepy waters of the open sea.

In silence they waited for the apparition. Slightly emotional at this end to a fine day, they watched the sun sinking little by little, like an enormous meteor. Suddenly Miss Campbell let out an involuntary cry. This was followed by an anxious exclamation, which neither the Melville brothers nor Oliver Sinclair were able to repress.

A launch was at that moment passing by the isle of Easdale, at the foot of Seil, and was slowly advancing towards the west. Its sail was spread out like a screen and stood up above the horizon. Would it hide the sun as it was extinguished in the waves?

It was a matter of seconds. There was no longer time for them to retrace their steps or to rush to one side or the other in order to find another location opposite the point of contact; the narrowness of the headland did not enable them to find an angle that was sufficient to put them back on the sun's axis.

Miss Campbell, driven to despair at this contretemps, was walking to and fro on the rocks. Oliver Sinclair was making tremendous gestures to the occupants of the boat and was shouting to them to draw in their sail.

But all in vain! They couldn't see him and they couldn't hear him. The launch, under the influence of a light breeze, continued to drift towards the west with the waves that carried it.

Just as the upper edge of the solar disc was about to disappear, the sail passed before it and hid it behind its opaque trapezium.

What a let-down! This time the Green Ray had been launched from the foot of this cloudless horizon, but it had collided with the sail before reaching the promontory on which so many eyes were watching for it avidly.

Miss Campbell, Oliver Sinclair and the Melville brothers, utterly disappointed, and more irritated perhaps than this mischance warranted, remained stunned in their places, forgetting even to leave, cursing the launch and those who were in it.

Meanwhile, the launch had drawn alongside a small cove in the isle of Seil, at the very base of the promontory.

At that moment a passenger got out, leaving on board the two sailors who had brought him across from the isle of Luing by sea. He then skirted around the shore and scaled the first rocks in order to reach the edge of the headland.

This intruder must certainly have recognised the group of observers stationed on the plateau, because he greeted them with a gesture tinged with a degree of familiarity.

'Mr Ursiclos! cried Miss Campbell.

'Him! It was him!' responded the brothers.

'Who can this gentleman be?' Oliver Sinclair said to himself.

It was indeed Aristobulus Ursiclos himself, who was returning after a scientific tour of some days from the isle of Luing.

There is no point in dwelling on how he was received by those who he had just disrupted in the realisation of their most cherished desire.

Brother Sam and brother Sib, forgetting all etiquette, did not even think of introducing Oliver Sinclair and Aristobulus Ursiclos to one another. Faced with Helena's displeasure, they looked down so as not to see the suitor of their choice.

Miss Campbell, her small hands clenched, her arms crossed on her breast, and her eyes flashing, looked at him without saying a

Oliver was making tremendous gestures…

word. Then, finally, the following words escaped her mouth: 'Mr Ursiclos, it would have been better if you had not arrived just at the right time to commit a blunder!'

12

New Plans

THE RETURN TO OBAN took place in much less agreeable circumstances than the journey to the isle of Seil had. They had set out expecting success, and were coming back with a defeat.

If Miss Campbell's disappointment could be mollified by one thing, it was because Aristobulus Ursiclos was the cause of it. She had the right to blame one who was so guilty, and to heap curses on his head. She didn't fail to do so. It would not have been fitting for the Melville brothers to try to defend him. No! The vessel of this clumsy man, to whom they had not given a thought, had had to arrive at the exact place where it would hide the horizon, at the moment when the sun launched its last luminous arrow. It was one of those things that can never be forgiven.

Needless to say that after this angry outburst Aristobulus Ursiclos, who had furthermore tried to excuse himself by mocking the Green Ray, had rejoined the launch for its return to Oban. He had acted wisely, for it is very likely that he would not have been offered a place in the coach, not even the seat at the back.

So it was that, for the second time, the sun had set in conditions in which it would have been possible to have seen the phenomenon, and that, for the second time, Miss Campbell's keen eyes had been exposed to the gleaming caresses of the star in vain, leaving her with blurred vision for several hours! First of all the rescue of Oliver Sinclair, and then the passage of Aristobulus

Ursiclos, had made her miss opportunities that would perhaps not recur for a long time! It is true that the circumstances had not been the same in the two cases, and that Miss Campbell excused the one as much as she blamed the other. Who could have accused her of partiality?

The following day, Oliver Sinclair was walking with a somewhat dreamy air on the shore at Oban.

Just who was this Mr Aristobulus Ursiclos? A relative of Miss Campbell and the Melville brothers, or simply a friend? He was evidently, at the very least, on familiar terms with the household, judging by the way in which Miss Campbell had allowed herself to reproach him for his blunder. Well, and what did it matter to Oliver Sinclair? If he wanted to know who he was dealing with, he only had to question brother Sam or brother Sib... And it was precisely this that he forbade himself to do, and thus that he didn't do.

And yet there were opportunities. Each day, Oliver Sinclair met the Melville brothers, sometimes out walking together – indeed, who could flatter themselves that they had seen one of them without the other –, sometimes accompanying their niece along the shore. They spoke of thousands of things, but especially of the weather, which, in the case in point, was not a way of talking about nothing. Would they ever find another of those serene evenings, whose return they watched for intently, when they would be able to go back to the isle of Seil? It seemed doubtful. In fact, since those two admirable slight improvements on the 2 and 14 August, the sky had been uncertain. There had been nothing but stormy clouds, horizons criss-crossed by summer lightening and fine drizzle at twilight, in short enough to drive an astronomy student, who was glued to the glass of his telescope and was seeking to revise a corner of the celestial map, to despair!

Why not confess that the young painter was now just as smitten with the Green Ray as Miss Campbell herself was? He had got on his hobbyhorse together with the beautiful young girl. With her he ran through the fields of space. He was riding this whim with no less ardour, not to mention with no less impatience than his young companion. Ah, he was not an Aristobulus Ursiclos, caught up in images of lofty science and full of disdain for a simple optical phenomenon! They understood one another, and they both wanted to be of that elite group of privileged people who the Green Ray has honoured with its appearance!

'We will see it, Miss Campbell,' repeated Oliver Sinclair, 'we will see it, even if I have to go and light it myself! All in all, it's my fault that it eluded you the first time, and I am as guilty as this Mr Ursiclos... a relation of yours, I believe?'

'No... my fiancé... it seems', Miss Campbell replied that day, walking off in some haste to rejoin her uncles, who were walking ahead, treating themselves to a pinch of snuff.

Her fiancé! It was strange the effect that this simple response had on Oliver Sinclair, and especially the tone in which it had been made! After all, why should this young pedant not be a fiancé? At least, in these circumstances, his presence in Oban was explained! That he had been unwise enough to come between Miss Campbell and the setting sun did not mean that... Did not mean what? Oliver Sinclair would perhaps have been very embarrassed to say.

Moreover, after an absence of two days Aristobulus Ursiclos had reappeared. Oliver Sinclair noticed him several times in the company of the Melville brothers, who would have been unable to hold it against him. He seemed to be on the very best of terms with them. The young scholar and the young artist had met on several occasions, either on the beach or in the lounges of the Caledonian Hotel. The two uncles had thought fit to introduce them to one another.

'Mr Aristobulus Ursiclos of Dumfries! Mr Oliver Sinclair of Edinburgh!'

This had occasioned a slight bow from each of the two young men, involving a simple nod of the head in which their inordinately straight bodies played no part. Evidently there would never be any love lost between these two characters. The one roamed the sky in search of stars, the other to calculate its components; the artist made no attempt to pose on the pedestal of art, the scientist made science into a pedestal for himself, and struck poses on it.

As for Miss Campbell, she refused to have anything to do

They spoke of thousands of things.

with Aristobulus Ursiclos. If he was there, she didn't seem to notice his presence; if he came to pass her, she visibly turned away. In a word, as has been explained before, she neatly 'cut' him in a formal British manner. The Melville brothers had some difficulty in reassembling the pieces. However that may be, they believed that everything would work out, especially if this capricious ray would finally appear.

In the meantime, Aristobulus Ursiclos watched Oliver Sinclair above his glasses – a familiar manoeuvre for all short-sighted people who want to look without seeming to. He saw the young man's assiduity to Miss Campbell, and the amiable welcome that the young girl gave him on every occasion. Doubtless neither was of a nature to please him, but, confident in himself, he remained reserved.

Meanwhile, the uncertain sky and the barometer, whose mobile needle never remained still, put the patience of all to a very long test. In the hope of finding a mist-free horizon, even if only for a few moments at sunset, they made two or three more excursions to the isle of Seil. Aristobulus Ursiclos didn't think fit to take part. But it was trouble in vain! The 23 August arrived and the phenomenon had not deigned to appear.

This whim became an idée fixe that left no room for any other. It turned into an obsession. They dreamed of it night and day, until it was to be feared that it was becoming a new type of monomania – in an era when they have become countless. In this frame of mind, all colours transformed themselves into one unique colour: the blue sky was green, the roads were green, the shore was green, the rocks were green, and the water and the wine were as green as absinthe. The Melville brothers imagined that they were dressed in green and mistook themselves for two large parrots, who took green snuff from a green snuffbox! In a word, it was a case of green madness! They were all struck by some sort of colour blindness, and oculists would have had matter for the publication of interesting notes in their ophthalmology reviews. It could not last much longer.

Luckily, Oliver Sinclair had an idea.

'Miss Campbell,' he said one day, 'and you gentlemen, it seems to me that, all things considered, we are not very well situated in Oban for the observation of the phenomenon in question.'

'And whose fault is that?' replied Miss Campbell, looking directly at the two guilty parties, who hung their heads.

'There is no marine horizon here!' resumed the young painter. 'Thus we are obliged to go to the isle of Seil to look for one, and risk not being there at the moment when we need to be!'

'That is obvious!' replied Miss Campbell. 'In fact, I don't know why my uncles chose this horrible place for our experiment!'

'Dear Helena!' replied brother Sam, not knowing what to say, 'We thought...'

'Yes... thought... the same thing...' added brother Sib, coming to his aid.

'That the sun would not fail to set on the horizon at Oban...'

'As Oban is situated on the coast!'

'And you thought wrong, uncles,' replied Miss Campbell, 'Very wrong, as it doesn't set here!

'Because,' resumed brother Sam, 'there are those annoying islands, which obstruct our view of the open sea!'

'You don't of course claim to be able to blow them up...' asked Miss Campbell.

'It would already have been done if it were possible', replied brother Sib in a decided tone.

'Nevertheless, we cannot go and camp on the isle of Seil', observed brother Sam.

'And why not?'

'Dear Helena, if you absolutely wish to...'

'Absolutely.'

'Let's leave then!' replied brother Sam and brother Sib in a resigned tone.

And those two docile creatures declared themselves ready to leave Oban immediately.

Oliver Sinclair intervened.

'Miss Campbell,' he said, 'unless you really want to, I think that we could do better than going to stay on the isle of Seil.'

'Speak out Mr Sinclair, and if your idea is better, my uncles will not refuse to follow it!'

The Melville brothers bowed their assent with an automatic movement so identical that they had perhaps never looked so alike.

'The isle of Seil', resumed Oliver Sinclair, 'is not really such that you can stay on it, even if only for a few days. If your patience has to be tried, Miss Campbell, it is not necessary that it is to the detriment of your well-being. I have, moreover, observed that the view of the sea is somewhat limited at Seil due to the shape of the coast. If, by some mishap, we have to wait longer than we think, if our stay should be extended by several weeks, it could be that the sun, which is now retrograding towards the west, would end up setting behind the island of Colonsay or the island of Oronsay, or even the large island of Islay, and our observation would once again fail for want of a large enough horizon.'

'Really,' replied Miss Campbell, 'that would be the final stroke of bad luck...'

'Which we can avoid by looking for a place situated further out of the Hebridean archipelago, and in front of which the whole of the Atlantic extends.'

'And do you know of such a place, Mr Sinclair?' Miss Campbell asked eagerly.

The Melville brothers were hanging on the young man's every word. What would he reply? Where the devil was their niece's whim going to end up leading them? What extremity in the continents of the Old World would they have to settle in to satisfy her desire?

Oliver Sinclair's reply had the effect of reassuring them straightaway.

'Miss Campbell,' he said, 'not far from here is a place that appears to me to offer every favourable condition. It is situated beyond the heights of Mull, which block the horizon to the west of Oban. It is one of the small Hebridean islands and is situated furthest out into the Atlantic; it is the charming island of Iona.'

'Iona!' cried Miss Campbell, 'Iona, uncles! Why are we not there yet?'

'We will be there tomorrow', replied brother Sam.

'Tomorrow before sunset', added brother Sib.

'Let's leave then,' resumed Miss Campbell, 'and if, on Iona, we don't find a wide, open expanse of water, take note uncles, we will look for another point on the coast, from John O'Groats, in the extreme north of Scotland, to Land's End at the southern tip of England, and if that is still not enough...'

'It is very simple,' replied Oliver Sinclair, 'we will go round the world!'

13

The Glories of the Sea

THE OWNER OF THE Caledonian Hotel showed signs of despair upon learning of his guests' decision. Had he been able to, Mr MacFyne would have had all the isles and islands that mask the view from the coast at Oban blown up. It may be added that, as soon as the family had left, he consoled himself by expressing his regrets at ever having accommodated such a group of monomaniacs.

At eight o'clock in the morning, the Melville brothers, Miss Campbell, dame Bess and Partridge boarded the 'swift steamer the *Pioneer*', as the brochure said, which makes the trip around the Isle of Mull with stops at Iona and Staffa, and then returns to Oban the same evening.

Oliver Sinclair had gone ahead of his companions to the landing stage, and was waiting for them on the bridge, between the steamer's two paddle drums.

Aristobulus Ursiclos was not even considered for this trip. The Melville brothers had however thought proper to warn him of their sudden departure. Mere politeness required this step, and they were the politest gentlemen in the world.

Aristobulus Ursiclos had received the communication offered by the two uncles fairly coolly, and had contented himself by simply thanking them without referring to his own plans.

The Melville brothers had thus retired, repeating to themselves that, though their protégé remained extremely reserved and though Miss Campbell had taken somewhat of an aversion to him, it would all change at the end of some beautiful autumn evening, after one of those beautiful sunsets that the isle of Iona would be full of. That was their opinion at least.

When all the passengers were on board and the steam whistle had erupted for the third time, the moorings were cast off and the *Pioneer* headed out of the bay, taking the Sound of Kerrera to the south.

There were a large number of tourists on board, of the kind who were attracted by this charming twelve hour excursion around the Isle of Mull two or three times a week, but Miss Campbell and her companions were to abandon them at the first port of call.

In fact they were longing to reach Iona, this new field for their observations. The weather was superb; the sea was as calm as a lake. The crossing would be beautiful. If that evening did not lead to the realisation of their desire, well, they would wait patiently after having settled on the island. There the curtain would be raised at least, and the scenery would always be in place. Only bad weather would cause there to be no performance.

To cut a long story short, they were to reach their destination before midday. The speedy *Pioneer* made its way down the Sound of Kerrera, rounded the southern point of the island, raced through the large opening into the Firth of Lorn, leaving behind Colonsay and its old abbey, which was founded by the famous Lords of the Isles in the fourteenth century, on its left, and sailed along the southern coast of Mull, lying washed up in the open sea like an immense crab, whose inner pincer curves slightly towards the south-west. At one moment, Ben More was visible at a height of 3,500 feet above the grim and steep hills in the distance, clothed naturally in heather, its rounded summit towered above those pastures, dotted with cows, abruptly divided by the imposing mass of Ardalanish Point.

Picturesque Iona stood out in the north-west, almost at the end of Mull's southern pincer. The Atlantic Ocean, immense and infinite, stretched out beyond.

'Do you like the ocean, Mr Sinclair?' Miss Campbell asked her young companion, who was sitting by her on the bridge of the *Pioneer*, contemplating the beautiful spectacle.

The *Pioneer* headed out of the bay, taking the Sound of Kerrera.

'Do I like it, Miss Campbell!' he replied. 'Yes, and I am not one of those unworthy people, who find the sight of it monotonous! In my eyes, nothing is more charming than its appearance, but you need to be able to watch it in its various phases. In fact, the sea is made up of so many shades so marvellously blended with one another that it is perhaps more difficult for a painter to reproduce the general effect of it, which is both uniform and varied at the same time, than it is for them to paint a face, however mobile its expression might be.'

'Indeed,' said Miss Campbell, 'it changes incessantly with the slightest breeze that passes, and alters at all hours of the day according to the light that impregnates it.'

'Look at it at this moment, Miss Campbell!' resumed Oliver Sinclair. 'It is absolutely calm! Does it not appear like a beautiful sleeping face, the admirable purity of which nothing can alter? It doesn't have a wrinkle, it is young, it is beautiful! Or, if you prefer, it is nothing but an immense mirror, but a mirror that reflects the sky and in which God can see himself!'

'A mirror that is too often tarnished by the stormy winds!' added Miss Campbell.

'Ah!' resumed Oliver Sinclair, 'That is what creates the ocean's vast variety of appearances! When a little wind gets up, the face changes, it grows wrinkly, the swell gives it white hair, it ages in an instant, it becomes a hundred years older, but it still remains superb with its capricious phosphorescence and its foam embroidery!'

'Do you think, Mr Sinclair', asked Miss Campbell, 'that any painter, however great he is, could ever reproduce all the beauties of the sea on canvas?'

'I don't think so, Miss Campbell. How could he? The sea does not really have its own colour. It is only an immense echo of the sky! Is it blue? It cannot be painted blue! Is it green? It cannot be painted green! It is easier to capture in its fury, when it is sombre, livid, nasty, when it seems that the sky mixes into it all the clouds that it keeps suspended above! Oh, Miss Campbell, the more I see of this ocean, the more I think it sublime! Ocean! The word says it all! It is immensity! It covers limitless prairies at unimaginable depths, beside which our own grassland is like a desert, as Darwin said. What are the greatest continents compared with it? Mere islands that it surrounds with its waters! It covers four fifths of the globe! By a sort of incessant circulation – like a living creature whose heart beat is the equator – it nourishes itself with the vapours it emits, with which it feeds its springs, and which flow back to it in rivers, or which it takes back directly through the rain that left its breast! Yes, the ocean is the infinite. It is an infinity that is not seen but that is felt, as one of the poets said, it is as infinite as the space that it reflects in its waters!'

'I like to hear you speak with such enthusiasm, Mr Sinclair', replied Miss Campbell, 'and I share your enthusiasm! Yes! I love the sea as you love it!'

'And you don't fear braving its perils?' asked Oliver Sinclair.

'No, indeed, I wouldn't be afraid. Is it possible to fear what you admire?'

'You would have made a hardy traveller?'

'Perhaps Mr Sinclair', replied Miss Campbell. 'In any case, of all the journeys about which I have read, I prefer those whose purpose was to discover distant seas. How many times I've crossed them with the great navigators! How many times I've launched myself into the great unknown – only in thought it is true; but I know nothing more enviable than the destiny of the heroes who have accomplished such great things!'

'Yes, Miss Campbell, in the entire history of humanity what is more beautiful than those discoveries! What a dream to cross the Atlantic for the first time with Columbus, the Pacific with Magellan, the polar seas with Parry, Franklin, d'Urville and so many others! I can't see a ship; warship, trading ship or a simple fishing boat leaving without my whole being climbing on board! I believe that I was made to be a sailor, and I regret every day that it has not been my career since childhood!'

'But you have at least travelled by sea?' asked Miss Campbell,

'As much as I have been able to', replied Oliver Sinclair. 'I have visited the Mediterranean a little, from Gibraltar to the ports of the Levant, the Atlantic a little as far as North America, and the northern seas of Europe, and I know all the waters that nature has lavished so liberally on both England and Scotland...'

'And so magnificently, Mr Sinclair!'

'Yes Miss Campbell, and I know nothing to compare with these Hebridean waters, on which this steamer is carrying us! It is a true archipelago, with a sky less blue than that of the Orient, but with more poetry perhaps in the combination of its wild rocks and its misty horizons. The Greek archipelago gave birth to a whole society of gods and goddesses. True! But you will remark that they were very bourgeois, very pragmatic divinities, gifted above all with a material life, carrying out their business and keeping a record of their spending. In my view, Olympia appears like a more or less well-selected salon where gods, who resemble men a little too much and with whom they share all their weaknesses, meet! It is not so in our Hebrides. It is the seat of supernatural beings! The Scandinavian deities are immaterial and ethereal with elusive forms, not bodies! They are Odin, Ossian, Fingal, and the entire host of poetic phantoms who escaped from the books of the Sagas! How beautiful are these figures, whose apparition can be invoked by our memory, in the midst of the mist of the Arctic seas, through the snows of hyperborean regions! Here is an Olympus that is far more divine than the Greek Olympus! The former has nothing earthly about it, and if it was necessary to assign it a place worthy of its guests, it would be in our Hebridean seas! Yes, Miss Campbell, it is here that I would come to worship our divinities, and as a true son of old Caledonia, I would not swap our archipelago with its two hundred islands, its sky laden with mist and its resonant tides, which are heated up by the currents of the Gulf Stream, for all the archipelagos in the eastern seas!'

'And it really belongs to us Highlanders!' replied Miss Campbell, carried away by the ardent words of her young companion. 'Ours, the Scots from the county of Argyll! Oh, Mr Sinclair, like you I am passionate about our Caledonian archipelago! It is superb, and I love it even when it is raging!'

'It is indeed sublime then', replied Oliver Sinclair. 'Nothing

'The sea...A chemical combination...'

can obstruct the violence of the gales that fling themselves at us, after having travelled three thousand miles! The coast of America faces Scotland! If it is there, on the other side of the Atlantic, that the great ocean storms are born, it is here in Western Europe that the first onslaught of the waves and the wind is unleashed! But what can they do against our Hebrides, which are more audacious than that man of whom Livingstone speaks, who was not afraid of lions, but who did fear the ocean, these islands, which stand firm on their granite bases and laugh at the violence of the wind and the sea!'

'The sea... a chemical combination of hydrogen and oxygen with two and a half percent sodium chloride! Nothing, in fact, is as beautiful as the raging of sodium chloride!'

Miss Campbell and Oliver had turned around on hearing these words, which had evidently been spoken for their benefit and pronounced in response to their enthusiasm.

Aristobulus Ursiclos was there on the bridge.

That irksome individual had been unable to resist leaving Oban at the same time as Miss Campbell, knowing that Oliver Sinclair would accompany her to Iona. So, he had boarded before them and, after remaining in the *Pioneer*'s lounge during the whole crossing, he had just come out again now the island was in sight.

The raging of sodium chloride! What a blow to the dreams of Oliver Sinclair and Miss Campbell!

14

Life on Iona

IN THE MEANTIME, Iona – or to give it its old name the Isle of the Waves – and its Hill of the Abbot, which rises no higher than 400 feet above sea level, grew more and more clear as the steamer approached it rapidly.

Towards midday, the *Pioneer* drew alongside a small jetty made of roughly hewn rocks, all of which had been turned green by the water. The passengers disembarked. Many of them would take to the sea again an hour later and return to Oban via the Sound of Mull, a lesser number – we know who – intended to remain on Iona.

The island does not have a port as such. A stone quay protects one of its inlets from the waves coming in off the open sea. That's it. It is here that several pleasure yachts and the fishing boats that work these waters shelter during the summer.

Miss Campbell and her companions, leaving the tourists to the mercy of an agenda that obliges them to see the island in two hours, occupied themselves with the search for a suitable dwelling.

It was not to be expected that the level of comfort found in the rich bathing resorts of the United Kingdom would be available on Iona.

In fact, Iona measures only three miles in length and one mile in width, and has scarcely five hundred inhabitants. The Duke of Argyll, to whom it belongs, only draws from it a revenue of several hundred pounds. There is no town as such there, nor even a small town or a village. Several scattered houses, for the most part simple dilapidated affairs, which could be said to be picturesque but are rudimentary, almost all without windows, the only light coming from the door, with only a hole in the roof for a chimney, having only pebble and mulch walls, thatch roofs made of reeds and heather bound together with large strands of wrack.

Who would have believed that Iona was the cradle of the Druid religion in the early part of Scandinavian history? Who would have imagined that after them, in the sixth century, St Columba – the Irishman whose name it also bears – founded the first monastery in the whole of Scotland there, in order to teach the new religion of Christ, and that the monks of Cluny lived there until the Reformation! Where are the vast buildings now, which were effectively the seminary of the bishops and great abbots of the United Kingdom? In the midst of the debris, where is the library, rich in records of the past and in manuscripts relating to Roman history, and from which the scholars of the period came to draw useful knowledge? No, at the present moment there are only ruins in the birthplace of the civilisation that was to change Europe so profoundly. From the St Columba of the past, there remains only the Iona of the present: a few rough peasants who extract a mediocre crop of barley, potatoes and wheat with difficulty from its sandy earth, and a few fishermen whose fishing boats eke a living out of the rich seas of the Hebrides!

'Miss Campbell', said Aristobulus Ursiclos in a disdainful tone, 'at first sight, do you think this place is equal to Oban?'

'It is better!' replied Miss Campbell, although she no doubt thought that there was one inhabitant too many on the isle.

In the meantime, as there were no villas or hotels, the Melville brothers had discovered a sort of inn that was almost passable. It was the place where tourists usually stayed if they were not content with the time the boat allowed for visiting the Druidic and Christian ruins of Iona. They were thus able to settle in the *Duncan's Arms* that very day, whilst Oliver Sinclair and Aristobulus Ursiclos took the best lodgings they could find in fishermen's huts.

But such was Miss Campbell's frame of mind that she was as happy in her small room, with its window looking out over the sea to the west, as she was on the terrace of the high tower in

'Would you like some 'sowens'...?'

Helensburgh, and certainly happier than in the lounge of the Caledonian Hotel. From there, the horizon stretched out before her eyes without any island to break its circular line, and with a little imagination she might have seen the American coast, 3,000 miles away on the other side of the Atlantic. The sun really did have a beautiful theatre there in which to set in all its splendour!

Their communal life was thus organised easily and simply. Meals were taken together in the inn's humble room. In accordance with the old custom, dame Bess and Partridge sat at their masters' table. Perhaps Aristobulus Ursiclos felt somewhat surprised by the fact, but Oliver Sinclair found no fault with it. He had already gained a sort of affection for these two servants, which they returned.

There the family led the old Scottish life in all its simplicity. After walks on the island and conversations on times past, into which Aristobulus Ursiclos never failed to hurl his modern notes at an inopportune moment, they came together again for midday dinner and for supper at eight o'clock in the evening. Then Miss Campbell would watch the sun setting whatever the weather, even when it was cloudy. Who knows! A break might appear low in the clouds, some crack or gap that would let the Green Ray through!

And what meals they had! The most Caledonian of Walter Scott's guests, at a dinner given by Fergus MacGregor, at or a supper given by Oldbuck the antiquary, would have found nothing to criticise in the dishes prepared after the fashion of old Scotland. Dame Bess and Partridge, taken back a century, felt as happy as if they had lived in the time of their ancestors. Brother Sam and brother Sib welcomed with evident pleasure the culinary combinations that had formerly been in use in the Melville family.

Here are the words that were spoken in that humble room, which had been transformed into a dining room.

'Would you like a few of these oatcakes, which taste so very different from the soft cakes in Glasgow?'

'Would you like some 'sowens', which the mountain dwellers in the Highlands still enjoy?'

'Do have some more haggis, which our great poet Burns

worthily celebrated in his verses as the first, the best and the most national of Scottish puddings!'

'Do have some more cockaleekie! Although the chicken is a little tough, the leeks with which it is prepared are excellent!'

'And a third helping of this hotchpotch, which is better than any of the cook's soups at Helensburgh!'

Ah, they ate well at the *Duncan's Arms*, which was stocked up every two days from the pantries of the steamers that serve the small Hebridean islands! And they drank well too!

You should have seen the Melville brothers toasting one another in moderation, glasses in hand, drinking to each other's health with those great quarts that contain no less than four English pints, and in which foamed the 'usquebaugh', the national beer par excellence, or better still 'hummock', brewed specially for them! And the whisky, extracted from barley, which seems to go on fermenting in the stomachs of the drinkers! And had there been a lack of strong beer, would they not have been content with simple 'mum', distilled from wheat, even if it was only the 'two penny' variety, which can always be embellished with a small glass of gin! To tell the truth, they hardly remembered to miss the sherry and port in the cellars at Helensburgh and Glasgow.

And although Aristobulus Ursiclos, who was used to modern comforts, did not fail to complain more often than was suitable, no-one paid any attention to his complaints.

Although he thought that time passed slowly on this isle, it passed quickly for the others, and Miss Campbell no longer complained bitterly about the mists that clouded the horizon each evening.

Iona is certainly not large, but are vast spaces necessary to people who like walking in the fresh air? Cannot the expanses of a royal park fit into a bit of garden? Thus they walked. Oliver Sinclair made sketches of several sites here and there. Miss Campbell watched him paint and thus the time passed.

The 26, 27, 28 and 29 August followed on from one another without a moment of boredom. This wild life was in keeping with this wild island, whose desolate rocks were battered relentlessly by the sea.

Miss Campbell, happy to have got away from the curious, talkative, inquisitive world of the bathing resorts, went out as she would have done in the park at Helensburgh, with her 'rokelay' wrapped around her like a mantilla, wearing in her hair a 'snod' or ribbon, of the type that gets caught up in the hair and that suits young Scottish girls so well. Oliver Sinclair never tired of admiring her grace, her charming person, and her appealing way, which produced on him an effect of which he was, moreover, well aware. Often the two of them would wander along, talking, watching, dreaming, to the furthest shores of the isle, trampling down the wrack brought in with the sea's last movements. Whole flocks of Scottish divers would fly up before them, 'tammie norries' disturbed in their solitude, 'pictarnies' on the look out for the little fish brought up by the swirl of the surf, and gannets with white feathers, black wing tips and yellow heads and throats, which are particular representatives of the class of palmipeds found in Hebridean ornithology.

Then, when evening came, after the sunset which was invariably veiled by mist, what a pleasure it was for Miss Campbell and her companions to pass the early hours of the night together on some deserted shore! Stars appeared the horizon, and with them returned many memories of Ossian's poems. In the midst of the profound silence, Miss Campbell and Oliver Sinclair would hear the two brothers reciting alternative stanzas by the ancient bard, the ill-fated son of Fingal.

> Star of the descending night! fair is thy light in the west! thou that liftest thy unshorn head from thy cloud: thy steps are stately on thy hill. What dost thou behold in the plain? The stormy winds are laid. The murmur of the torrent comes from afar. Roaring waves climb the distant rock. The midges of evening are on their feeble wings, and the hum of their course is on the field. What dost thou behold, fair light? But thou dost smile and depart. The waves come with joy around thee, and bathe thy lovely hair. Farewell, thou silent beam!

Then brother Sam and brother Sib would fall silent, and they would all return to their small room in the inn.

Meanwhile, as short-sighted as the Melville brothers were, they saw that what Aristobulus Ursiclos lost in Miss Campbell's thoughts, Oliver Sinclair gained. The two young men avoided each other as much as possible. Thus the uncles occupied themselves, and not without some difficulty, with reuniting the small group and with bringing about a reconciliation at the risk of some sally from their niece. Yes, they would have been happy to see Ursiclos and Sinclair seeking each other's company, instead of avoiding each other and maintaining a disdainful reserve when together. Did they think that all men are brothers, and brothers in the manner in which they themselves were?

Finally, they managed things so adroitly that, on the 30 August, it was agreed that they would go together to visit the ruins of the church, monastery and cemetery, which were situated to the north-east and to the south of the hill of the Abbot. This walk, which takes tourists barely two hours, had not yet been undertaken by Iona's new guests. It showed a lack of propriety regarding the legendary shadows of those hermit monks who then lived in the huts along the coast, and a lack of respect for the illustrious dead of the royal families from Fergus II to Macbeth.

15

The Ruins of Iona

ON THAT DAY, Miss Campbell, the Melville brothers and the two young men thus set out after lunch. It was a fine autumn day. Every so often gleams of light would filter through gaps in the thin clouds. Under these intermittent rays, the ruins crowning that part of the isle, the picturesque groups of rocks on the coast, the houses scattered upon the rough Iona land, and the sea, rippling in the distance under the caresses of a gentle breeze, seemed to alter their somewhat sad appearance and to brighten up in the sun.

It was not the day for visitors. The steamer had deposited fifty of them the day before, it would doubtless deposit just as many the following day, but today the island of Iona belonged entirely to its new inhabitants. The ruins would thus be absolutely deserted when the walkers arrived there.

They made their way there gaily. The good humour of the brothers Sam and Sib had won over their companions. They chatted, walking to and fro and wandering along the small rocky paths between low walls of dry stone.

Everything was thus going well when they stopped in front of MacLean's Cross. This beautiful monolith of red granite is 14 feet high and overlooks the road of Main Street. It is the sole survivor of the three hundred and sixty crosses that were scattered over the island until the time of the Reformation towards the middle of the sixteenth century.

Oliver Sinclair wanted to make a sketch of this monument, and with good reason for it is fine work and has a beautiful effect in the midst of an arid plain carpeted with greying grass.

He was attacking it with blows from his hammer.

Miss Campbell, the Melville brothers and he thus stood in a group around 50 feet away from the cross, so as to get a view of its entirety. Oliver Sinclair sat down on the corner of a small wall and began to draw the foreground of the area on which MacLean's Cross stands.

Some moments later, it seemed to them all that a human form was having a go at climbing up the base of the cross.

'Well!' said Oliver Sinclair, 'what can this intruder want here? If he was dressed as a monk, he wouldn't stick out like a sore thumb, and I could draw him prostrate at the foot of this ancient cross!'

'It's simply some inquisitive person who will be in your way, Mr Sinclair', replied Miss Campbell.

'But is it not Aristobulus Ursiclos, who has got ahead of us?' said brother Sam.

'It is he!' added brother Sib.

And indeed it was Aristobulus Ursiclos. He had got up onto the base of the cross and was attacking it with blows from his hammer.

Miss Campbell, outraged by the mineralogist's lack of consideration, ran towards him straight away: 'What are you doing sir?' she asked.

'As you can see, Miss Campbell,' Aristobulus Ursiclos replied, 'I am trying to remove a piece of this granite.'

'But what is this madness in aid of? I thought that the era of iconoclasts had passed!'

'I am not an iconoclast,' replied Aristobulus Ursiclos, 'but I am a geologist and, as such, I would like to know the nature of this stone.'

A violent blow from his hammer finished off the defacement, and a piece of stone from the base rolled to the ground.

Aristobulus Ursiclos picked it up and, doubling the optical power of his glasses with a large naturalist's magnifying glass which he drew from his case, he peered at it closely.

'It is as I thought', he said. 'It is very strong red granite with a very dense grain, which must have been extracted from Nun's Island, very similar to that with which the twelfth century architects constructed Iona's cathedral.'

And Aristobulus Ursiclos did not waste such a wonderful opportunity of launching into an archaeological lecture, which the Melville brothers – who had just joined them – thought fit to listen to.

Miss Campbell, without further ceremony, had returned to Oliver Sinclair and, when the drawing was finished, they all met again in the square in front of the cathedral.

This monument is a complex edifice made up of two connected churches, with walls as thick as curtain walls and with pillars solid as rocks, which have braved the assault of the climate for thirteen hundred years.

For some minutes, the visitors walked around in the first church, which is Norman in the arch of its vaults and the curve of its arches, then in the second, a Gothic edifice from the twelfth century forming the nave and transepts of the first. They went thus, through the ruins, from one period to another, walking upon the large square stones, through the cracks of which soil could be seen. Scattered around were the covers of tombs, whilst several gravestones stood in corners, their sculpted figures seeming to await alms from the passer-by.

The whole place, heavy, severe and silent, exuded the poetry of past eras.

Miss Campbell, Oliver Sinclair and the Melville brothers, failing to notice that their over learned companion was lagging behind, passed under the thick vault of the square tower – a vault that had once towered above the door of the first church and that later became the intersecting point of the two buildings.

Some moments later, measured steps could be heard on the sonorous pavement. You would have been forgiven for thinking that a stone statue, brought to life by the breath of some spirit, was walking heavily, like the Commander in the salon of Don Juan.

It was Aristobulus Ursiclos, who, with his metric strides, was measuring the dimensions of the cathedral: 'One hundred and sixty feet from east to west', he said, noting the figure in his notebook as he entered the second church.

'Oh, it's you, Mr Ursiclos!' said Miss Campbell sarcastically. 'After the mineralogist comes the geometrician?'

Aristobulus Ursiclos and his metric strides.

'And only 70 feet where the transepts cross', replied Aristobulus Ursiclos.

'And how many inches?' asked Oliver Sinclair.

Aristobulus Ursiclos looked at Oliver Sinclair as if he didn't know whether to be angry or not. But the Melville brothers, intervening at an opportune moment, carried off Miss Campbell and the two young men to visit the monastery.

All that is left of this building are unrecognisable remains, even though it survived the defacement it suffered in the Reformation. After this period, it was even used by a community of Augustinian canonesses to whom the state gave asylum there. All that remains now are the miserable ruins of a convent, devastated by storms, having no semi-circular vault or Roman pillars with which to resist with impunity the bad weather of a far northern climate.

However, after exploring what remained of the monastery, formerly so flourishing, the visitors were still able to admire the chapel, which was better conserved, and whose interior dimensions Aristobulus Ursiclos felt no necessity of measuring. In this chapel, which was either less ancient or more solidly constructed than the refectories and the cloisters of the convent, only the roof was missing, and the choir, which is almost intact, is a piece of architecture very much admired by antiquaries.

It is in the western part that the tomb of the last abbess of the community stands. On the slab of black marble appears a virgin's face, sculpted between two angels, and above a Madonna holding the baby Jesus in her arms.

'Just like the seated Virgin and the Madonna of St Sextus, the only Virgins by Raphael who don't have their eyelids lowered. This one is watching and it appears that her eyes are smiling!'

This very appropriate remark was made by Miss Campbell, but it brought a somewhat sarcastic pout to Aristobulus Ursiclos' lips.

'Where have you got the idea, Miss Campbell,' he said, 'that eyes can ever smile?'

Perhaps Miss Campbell would have liked to have replied that, in any case, her eyes would never have that expression when looking at him, but she kept silent.

'It is a widespread error,' resumed Aristobulus Ursiclos, as if he were speaking *ex cathedra,* 'to speak of eyes smiling. These organs of sight are devoid of all expression, as oculists teach us. For example, put a mask over a face, look at the eyes through the mask, and I defy you to know whether the face is gay, sad or angry.'

'Really?' replied brother Sam, who seemed interested in this short lesson.

'I wasn't aware of that', added brother Sib.

'Yet it is so,' resumed Aristobulus Ursiclos, 'and if I had a mask...'

But the surprising young man did not have a mask, and the experiment could not be carried out so as to remove all doubt in this respect.

Moreover, Miss Campbell and Oliver Sinclair had already left the cloister, and were heading towards the Iona cemetery.

This place bears the name of the 'Reliquary of Oban' in memory of St Columba's companion, to whom we owe the construction of the chapel whose ruins stand in the midst of this field of the dead.

It is a curious place, this piece of ground scattered with gravestones, where lie forty-eight Scottish kings, eight viceroys of the Hebrides, four viceroys of Ireland, and one king of France, his name lost like that of some leader in prehistoric times. Surrounded by its long iron railings, paved with slabs placed side by side, it looks like a sort of field in Carnac, whose stones are tombs and not druidic rocks. Between them, sleeping on the green bed, is laid out the granite figure of Duncan, King of Scotland, who was made famous in the sombre tragedy of *Macbeth*. Of these stones, some are ornamented simply with a geometric design, others, sculpted in the round, depict some of the ferocious Celtic kings, stretched out there with the rigidity of corpses.

How many memories there are hovering above this Iona necropolis! How your imagination retreats into the past when you scour the soil of this St Denis of the Hebrides!

And is it possible to forget Ossian's stanza, which seems to have been inspired by this very place?

Son of the distant land! Thou dwellest in the field of
fame! O, let thy song arise, at times, in praise of those
who fell. Let their thin ghosts rejoice around thee.

Miss Campbell and her companions looked on in silence. They
did not have to suffer the tedium of some official guide tearing
through the uncertainties of a history so far distant for a few
tourists. It appeared to them that they could see those descendents
of the Lord of the Isles, Angus Og, the companion of Robert the
Bruce, the brother in arms of this hero, who fought for the independence of his country.

'I would like to come here again at nightfall', said Miss
Campbell. 'It seems to me that it would be a more favourable
hour for recalling these memories. I would see them bringing the
body of the unfortunate Duncan. I would hear the words of those
burying him, as they laid him in the earth consecrated to his ancestors. Really, Mr Sinclair, would that not be the right moment to
conjure up the imps who guard the royal cemetery?'

'Yes, Miss Campbell, and I don't think they would fail to
appear at the sound of your voice.'

'What, Miss Campbell, you believe in imps?' cried
Aristobulus Ursiclos.

'I believe in them, sir, I believe in them like the good Scot that
I am', replied Miss Campbell.

'But really, you do know that it's all imaginary, that none of
this fantasy exists!'

'And what if I want to believe it!' replied Miss Campbell,
spurred on by this unwelcome contradiction. 'What if I want to
believe in domestic brownies who look after the furniture in houses,
in witches whose incantations are the declamation of runic verses, in
the Valkyries, those fatal virgins of Scandinavian mythology who
carry off warriors who fall in battle, in those household fairies of
whom our poet Burns sung in his immortal verses, which no true
Highlander can ever forget:

Upon that night, when fairies light
On Cassilis Downans dance,
Or owre the lays, in splendid blaze,
On sprightly coursers prance;
Or for Colean the route is ta'en,
Beneath the moon's pale beams;
There up the cove to stray and rove
Amang the rocks and streams
To sport that night.

'Ah, Miss Campbell,' continued the stubborn fool, 'do you really think that the poets believe in these dreams of their imagination?'

'Certainly sir,' replied Oliver Sinclair, 'or their poetry would sound false, as does any work that is not born from a profound conviction.'

'You too sir? replied Aristobulus Ursiclos. 'I knew you were a painter, I didn't know you were a poet.'

'It is the same thing', said Miss Campbell. 'Art is all one, but has various forms.'

'But no... no... it is inadmissible! You cannot believe in all the mythology of the ancient bards, whose troubled brains evoked imaginary divinities!'

'Oh, Mr Ursiclos!' cried brother Sam, cut to the quick, 'don't treat in such a way those of our ancestors who sung of our old Scotland!'

'Just listen to them!' said brother Sib, reverting to quotations from their favourite poem. 'Pleasant are the words of the song, and lovely are the tales of other times! They are like the calm dew of the morning on the hill...'

'When the sun is faint on its side, and the lake is settled and blue in the vale', added brother Sam.

No doubt the brothers would have continued indefinitely to indulge in the poetry of Ossian, had not Aristobulus Ursiclos abruptly interrupted them by saying: 'Sirs, have you ever seen one of these so-called spirits of which you speak so enthusiastically? No! And can they be seen? No, they can't, can they?'

Miss Campbell and her companions looked on in silence.

'That's where you are mistaken sir, and I pity you for never having noticed them', resumed Miss Campbell, who would not have yielded a hair of a single one of these imps to her opponent. 'You can see them throughout the highlands of Scotland, gliding along abandoned glens, rising from the bottom of ravines, flitting about on the surface of lakes, frolicking in the peaceful waters of our Hebrides, playing in the midst of the storms that the boreal winter throws at them. And look, why should not this Green Ray, which I am persisting in pursuing, be the scarf of some Valkyrie with its fringe trailing in the waters of the horizon?'

'Ah, no!' cried Aristobulus Ursiclos, 'not that! I will tell you what your Green Ray is.'

'Don't tell me, sir', cried Miss Campbell, 'I do not wish to know!'

'But I will', replied Aristobulus Ursiclos, completely aroused by the discussion.

'I forbid you...'

'I will tell you anyway, Miss Campbell. If this last ray, launched by the sun when the upper edge of its disc touches the horizon, is green, it is perhaps because, as it crosses the thin layer of water, it becomes impregnated with its colour...'

'Be quiet Mr Ursiclos!'

'Unless this green is the very natural successor of the red of the disc, which disappears suddenly, leaving an impression on our eye, because optically green is its complimentary colour!'

'Sir, your physical arguments...'

'My arguments, Miss Campbell, are in agreement with the nature of things,' replied Aristobulus Ursiclos, 'and I intend to publish a dissertation on the subject.'

'Let's leave, uncles!' cried Miss Campbell, thoroughly irritated. 'Mr Ursiclos and his explanations will end up ruining my Green Ray for me!'

Oliver Sinclair then intervened: 'Sir', he said, 'I think that your dissertation on the subject of the Green Ray would be extremely interesting, but allow me to propose another to you, on a subject that is perhaps even more interesting.'

'And what is that, sir?' asked Aristobulus Ursiclos, getting his hackles up.

'You must be aware, sir, that some scholars have handled scientifically the thrilling matter of 'The influence of fishes' tails on the undulations of the sea?'

'What, sir!'

'Well sir, here is another that I recommend particularly for your scholarly meditation: 'The influence of wind instruments on the formation of storms.'

16

Two Gun Shots

THE NEXT DAY, and during the first few days of September, they saw nothing of Aristobulus Ursiclos. Had he left Iona on the tourist boat, having understood that he was wasting his time with Miss Campbell? No-one could say. In any case, he did well not to appear. It was no longer merely indifference but a sort of aversion that he inspired in the young girl. To have taken the poetry out of her ray, to have materialized her dream, to have changed the scarf of a Valkyrie into a brutal optical phenomenon! Perhaps she would have forgiven him anything, anything except that.

The Melville brothers were not even allowed to go to enquire what had become of Aristobulus Ursiclos.

What good would it have done, anyway? What could they have said to him and what were they still hoping for? Could they henceforth dream of a planned union between two beings who were so out of sympathy with each other, and who were separated by the abyss that extends between vulgar prose and sublime poetry, the one with his mania for reducing everything to scientific formulas, the other living only in the ideal, which disdains causes and is content with impressions!

Meanwhile Partridge, urged on by dame Bess, learnt that this 'young old scholar', as he called him, had not yet made his departure and was still living in his fisherman's hut where he took his meals alone.

In any case, the important thing was that they no longer saw Aristobulus Ursiclos. The truth is, when he didn't confine himself to his room, busy no doubt with some lofty scientific speculation, he went around with his gun on his back along the low-lying shores of the coast, and there gave vent to his ill humour through the slaughtering of black mergansers or seagulls, which abounded there. Did he thus still retain some hope? Did he tell himself that, once her whim in relation to the Green Ray had been satisfied, Miss Campbell would return to a better frame of mind? It is after all possible, given her personality.

But one day a somewhat disagreeable adventure happened, which might have ended very badly for him without the generous and unexpected intervention of his rival.

It was the afternoon of the 2 September. Aristobulus Ursiclos had gone to study the rocks that form the most southerly tip of Iona. One of these granite stacks in particular attracted his attention, so much so that he resolved to heave himself up to its summit. Now it was a somewhat imprudent thing to do, as the rock was almost entirely made up of smooth surfaces and there were no footholds.

However, Aristobulus Ursiclos was not to be daunted. He thus began to climb the wall, using a few tufts of vegetation that grew here and there to help himself, and he was able to reach the summit of the stack, though not without some difficulty.

Once there he devoted himself to his usual pursuit of mineralogy, but when he tried to descend it became more difficult. In fact, after having looked carefully to see which side of the wall it would be best to slide down, he ventured upon it. At that moment his foot slipped, he tumbled down without being able to stop himself, and would have fallen into the violent waves of the surf had it not been for a broken stump that stopped him in the middle of his fall.

Aristobulus Ursiclos thus found himself in a situation that was both dangerous and ridiculous. He could not climb back up, but nor could he climb down.

An hour passed in this way, and who knows what would have happened had not Oliver Sinclair been passing by at that time, his painter's knapsack on his back. He heard shouts and stopped. Seeing Aristobulus Ursiclos hanging 30 feet up in the air, swinging

Oliver heard shouts and stopped.

to and fro like one of those wicker men suspended in the entrance of a tavern, at first made him want to laugh, but, as might be expected, he did not hesitate in going to get him down.

This was not an easy matter. Oliver Sinclair had to climb up to the top of the stack, haul the hanging man back up, and then help him to climb down again on the other side.

'Mr Sinclair,' said Aristobulus Ursiclos as soon as he was back in a safe place, 'I miscalculated the wall's angle of inclination from the vertical. Hence, I slipped and became suspended...'

'Mr Ursiclos,' replied Oliver Sinclair, 'I am happy that chance allowed me to come to your aid!'

'Allow me nonetheless to thank you...'

'There is no need, sir. You would certainly have done as much for me?'

'Undoubtedly.'

'Well, I will permit you to return the favour!'

And the two young men separated.

Oliver Sinclair did not think it necessary to speak of the incident, which was not particularly important. As for Aristobulus Ursiclos, he did not speak of it either, but at heart, as he valued his life, he was grateful to his rival for having got him out of this nasty situation.

And what of the famous ray? It must be admitted that it needed a singular amount of coaxing! Yet there was no more time to lose. Autumn would soon cover the sky with its veil of mist. Then there would be no more of those clear evenings that September is so miserly with at these elevated latitudes. No more of those clear horizons that seem as if they are traced by a geometrician's compass rather than by an artist's brush. Would they have to give up their quest to see this phenomenon, for which they had journeyed so far? Would they be obliged to postpone their observations until next year, or would they stubbornly persist in pursuing it under different skies?

To tell the truth, it was a cause of vexation for Miss Campbell as well as for Oliver Sinclair. They were both furious at seeing the Hebridean horizon obscured by mist from the open sea.

Such was the state of affairs for the first four days of the foggy month of September.

Every evening Miss Campbell, Oliver Sinclair, brother Sam, brother Sib, dame Bess and Partridge would sit down on some rock, washed by the slight undulations of the tide, and conscientiously watch the sun set against a brilliant background of light, more splendid undoubtedly than if the sky had been perfectly clear.

An artist would have danced for joy at these magnificent grand finales that developed at the end of the day, at this dazzling range of colours, shading off from one cloud to the next, from the violet of the zenith to the golden red of the horizon, at this dazzling cascade of fire bounding up off aerial rocks. But here the rocks were clouds, and these images, biting into the disk of the sun, absorbed its last rays, including the one that the eyes of the watchers were searching for in vain.

Then, once the sun had set, they all stood up, disappointed, like the spectators at an extravaganza whose final effect has been spoilt by the mistake of some stagehand. They then returned to the *Duncan's Arms* inn via the longest route.

'See you tomorrow', Miss Campbell would say.

'See you tomorrow', the two uncles replied. 'We have a sort of presentiment that tomorrow...'

And every evening the Melville brothers had a presentiment, which invariably finished in disappointment.

However, the 5 September began with a superb morning. The haze at sunrise melted away with the heat from the first rays of the sun.

The barometer, whose needle had been moving towards fine weather for some days, continued to rise and stopped at fair. It was no longer hot enough for the sky to be impregnated with that wavy mist of burning summer days. The dryness of the atmosphere was to be felt at sea level, just as it would have been felt on a mountain at several thousand feet of altitude in rarefied air.

It is impossible to say with what anxiety they all followed the changes of that day. We must abandon the idea of stating with what palpitations of the heart they watched when some cloud rose in the sky. It would be reckless to try to express with what anguish they followed the sun's trajectory in its diurnal march.

Luckily the breeze, slight but continuous, came off the land. By passing the mountains in the east and by gliding across the surface of the long meadows in the background, it ought not to become charged with the humid molecules that are emitted by vast expanses of water, and that are brought by winds from the open sea in the evening.

But how long it took the day to pass! Miss Campbell could not keep still. Braving the scorching heat, she walked to and fro, whilst Oliver Sinclair scoured the island's higher points looking for a more extensive horizon. The two uncles emptied a whole snuffbox between them, and Partridge, as if he were on guard duty, stood in the attitude of a rural policeman appointed to watch the celestial plains.

It had been agreed that they would dine at five o'clock that day, so as to be at their observation post early. The sun should not disappear until six forty-nine, and so they would have time to follow it until it set.

'I think we'll get it this time!' said brother Sam, rubbing his hands together.

'I think so too!' said brother Sib, performing the same act.

However, at about three o'clock, there was an alarm. A large fleck of cloud, the ghost of a cumulus, arose in the east and, carried by the breeze off the land, headed towards the ocean.

It was Miss Campbell who saw it first. She could not hold back an exclamation of disappointment.

'It's only the one cloud; we have nothing to fear', said one of the uncles. 'It will not be long in dissolving...'

'Or it will travel faster than the sun,' replied Oliver Sinclair, 'and will disappear beneath the horizon before it.'

'But isn't that cloud the forerunner of a bank of fog?' asked Miss Campbell.

'I'll see.'

And Oliver Sinclair ran to the ruins of the monastery. From there he could see further behind to the east above the mountains of Mull.

These mountains were very clearly outlined; their tops resembled a wavy line drawn with a pencil on a perfectly white background.

There was not another cloud in the sky, and no mist hung around Ben More's summit, which stood out clearly 3,000 feet above sea level.

Oliver Sinclair returned an hour later with reassuring words. This cloud was but a child lost in space; it would not even find anything to feed upon in this dry atmosphere, and would perish from hunger on its journey.

Meanwhile, the white fleck advanced towards the zenith. To the great displeasure of all, it followed the sun's path, coming nearer to it under the influence of the breeze. As it glided through the sky, its structure was altered in the eddy of the aerial current. From its initial shape, which resembled a dog's head, it took the form of a fish, some sort of gigantic ray, and then came together to form a ball, dark at the centre, dazzling at its edges, and, at that moment, reached the sun.

A cry escaped Miss Campbell, who stretched out her two arms towards the sky.

The radiant star, hidden behind this screen of haze, no longer sent a single one of its rays to the island. Iona, placed outside the zone of direct irradiation, was veiled in a large shadow.

But soon the large shadow moved. The sun reappeared in all its glory. The cloud sank towards the horizon. It was not even to reach it; half an hour later it vanished, as if some hole had been made in the sky.

'Finally it has gone,' cried the young girl, 'and I hope it won't be followed by another!'

'No, reassure yourself, Miss Campbell', replied Oliver Sinclair. 'If that cloud disappeared so quickly, and in such a manner, it shows it didn't meet any other vapour in the atmosphere, and that the sky to the west is absolutely clear.'

At six in the evening the spectators were at their post in an exposed location.

It was at the very south of the island on the highest point of the hill of the abbot. From this summit they could see the entire upper portion of Mull to the east. To the north, the isle of Staffa appeared like an enormous tortoise shell, washed up in the Hebridean waters. Beyond, Ulva and Gometra stood out from the long coastline of the large isle. Towards the west, the southwest and the northwest lay the immense sea.

The sun sank quickly on an oblique trajectory. The perimeter of the horizon formed a black line that you would have thought had been traced in Chinese ink. In the opposite direction, the windows of the houses on Iona were ablaze, as though reflecting a fire whose flames were flames of gold.

Miss Campbell and Oliver Sinclair, the Melville brothers, dame Bess and Partridge, gripped by this sublime spectacle, remained silent. With their eyes half closed, they watched the disc becoming deformed, swelling in parallel with the line of the water and taking the form of an enormous scarlet hot-air balloon. There was not a single wisp of vapour in the open sea.

'I think we'll manage it this time', brother Sam said again.

'I think so too', brother Sib replied.

'Silence, uncles!' cried Miss Campbell.

And they were silent, holding their breath as if they were afraid that it would condense into the form of a slight cloud, which might have veiled the disc of the sun.

The star's lower edge had finally bitten into the horizon. It grew larger and larger, as if it was filling with luminous liquid.

Their eyes seemed to draw in its last rays.

Like Arago, in the deserts of Palma on the Spanish coast, spying the light signal that was to appear at the summit of the isle of Ibiza and allow him to close the last triangle of his meridian!

Finally, all that remained of the disc above the water was a slight section of its upper arc. The supreme ray would be launched into the sky within the next fifteen seconds, presenting the eyes ready to receive it with that impression of a heavenly green!

Suddenly, two bangs echoed in the midst of the rocks on the shore below the hill. Some smoke rose up, and between its curls a cloud of seabirds flew up, seagulls, gulls and petrels, frightened by the untimely gun shots.

Following the flight of the birds with his eyes…

The cloud rose straight up, interposing itself like a screen between the horizon and the island, it passed before the dying sun just as it sent its last ray of light up from the surface of the water.

At that moment, on a headland on the edge of a cliff, they saw the inevitable Aristobulus Ursiclos, his smoking gun in his hand, following the flight of the birds with his eyes.

'Ah, this time, enough is enough!' cried brother Sib.

'It is too much!' cried brother Sam.

'I would have done well to leave him hanging on his rock,' Oliver Sinclair said to himself, 'at least he would still be there.'

Miss Campbell, her lips pursed, her eyes fixed, didn't say a single word.

Once more, and due to Aristobulus Ursiclos, she had missed the Green Ray!

17

On Board the *Clorinda*

THE NEXT DAY, at six in the morning, a charming 45 to 50-tonne yawl, the *Clorinda*, left the small port of Iona, and, under a light north-easterly breeze, on starboard tack, reached the open sea.

The *Clorinda* carried away Miss Campbell, Oliver Sinclair, brother Sam, brother Sib, dame Bess and Partridge.

It need not be said that the unfortunate Aristobulus Ursiclos was not on board.

This arrangement had been agreed on and immediately executed following the adventure of the previous evening.

On leaving the Hill of the Abbot to return to the inn, Miss Campbell had said abruptly: 'Uncles, as Mr Aristobulus Ursiclos intends to stay on in Iona, we will leave Iona to Mr Aristobulus Ursiclos. Once in Oban, a second time here, it has been his fault that our observations have not been able to be carried out. We will not stay a day longer in a place where this irksome individual has the privilege of making blunders!'

The Melville brothers had found nothing to say against this proposition, distinctly formulated as it was. Moreover, they too shared in the general feeling of discontent and cursed Aristobulus Ursiclos. Indeed, the situation of their suitor had been compromised forever. Nothing would bring Miss Campbell back to him. It was necessary to give up the accomplishment of a project that had become unrealisable.

'After all,' as brother Sam observed to brother Sib, who he had taken to one side, 'promises imprudently made are not iron handcuffs.'

In other words, this means that you can never be tied down by reckless oaths, and brother Sib, with a very clear gesture, gave his complete approbation to this Scottish saying.

When they parted for the night in the humble room at the *Duncan's Arms,* the conversation went as follows:

'We will leave tomorrow', Miss Campbell said. 'I will not remain here another day!'

'That's understood, my dear Helena,' replied brother Sam, 'but where will we go?'

'Anywhere where we are certain not to meet Mr Ursiclos! It is therefore important that no-one knows that we are leaving Iona, nor where we are going.'

'It is agreed,' replied brother Sib, 'but my dear girl, how will we travel and where will we go?'

'What!' cried Miss Campbell, 'Can we not find a way of leaving this isle at dawn? Is there not some uninhabited point, perhaps even uninhabitable, that the Scottish coast can offer us, where we will be able to pursue our experiment in peace?'

The two Melville brothers would certainly have been unable to respond to this double question, put to them in a tone that admitted no escape nor evasion.

Luckily, Oliver Sinclair was there.

'Miss Campbell,' he said, 'everything can be arranged as so. There is an island, or rather an isle, near here that is very suitable for our observations, and no irksome individual will come to disturb us on this isle.'

'Which is it?'

'Staffa, which you can see two miles to the north of Iona at the most.'

'Is there a way in which we can live there and is it possible to get there?'

'Yes,' replied Oliver Sinclair, 'and very easily. In the port of Iona, I have seen a yacht of the type always ready to take to the sea, as are to be found in all British ports during the summer. Its captain and crew are at the disposal of any tourist who wants to use their services to visit the Channel, the North Sea or the Irish Sea.

At six in the morning…

Well, what prevents us from chartering this yacht, from getting enough provisions on board for a fortnight, and from leaving tomorrow at the first light of day?'

'Mr Sinclair,' Miss Campbell replied, 'if we leave this island in secret tomorrow, believe me when I say I will be truly grateful to you.'

'Tomorrow, before midday, provided that a little breeze arises in the morning, we will be on Staffa,' replied Oliver Sinclair, 'and, except during the visit of tourists which lasts for barely an hour twice a week, we will not be disturbed by anyone.'

Following the Melville brothers' usual habit, the nicknames of their housekeeper resounded immediately.

'Bet!'

'Beth!'

'Bess!'

'Betsy!'

'Betty!'

Dame Bess appeared straightaway.

'We leave tomorrow!' said brother Sam.

'Tomorrow at dawn!' said brother Sib.

And at this, dame Bess and Partridge, without further ado, occupied themselves immediately with the preparations for the departure.

During this time, Oliver Sinclair headed for the port and there made arrangements with John Olduck.

John Olduck was the captain of the *Clorinda*, a real sailor with a small traditional cap with gold braid, dressed in a jacket with metal buttons and trousers of thick blue woollen cloth. Immediately after the deal had been concluded, he and his six men occupied themselves with making preparations for getting under way. His crew was composed of six of those choice sailors who are, by profession, fishermen during the winter, and who undertake the service of yachting during the summer, and do so in a manner that is undoubtedly superior to that of all sailors from other countries.

At six in the morning, the *Clorinda*'s new passengers embarked without having told anyone the destination of their yacht. They had collected together all the provisions they could get, including fresh and preserved meat and drinks. Moreover, the *Clorinda*'s cook would always have the resource of being able to stock up from the steamer that regularly made the trip from Oban to Staffa.

Thus, at dawn, Miss Campbell had taken possession of a charming and pretty room at the rear of the yacht. The two brothers occupied the bunks in the main cabin beyond the lounge, which was comfortably situated in the largest part of the small boat. Oliver Sinclair had a cabin under the main staircase that led to the lounge. On either side of the dining room, which was traversed by the foot of the mainmast, dame Bess and Partridge had two bunks, one on the right and the other on the left, behind the office and the captain's room. Further forward was the kitchen, where the master cook stayed. Further forward still were the crew's quarters, equipped with six hammocks. Nothing was wanting on this lovely yawl, which had been made by Ratsey of Cowes. With a fair sea and gentle breeze, it had always maintained an honourable rank in the Royal Thames Yacht Club regattas.

Everyone was delighted when the *Clorinda* cast off, raised her anchor and began to catch the wind in her big sail, jigger, foresail, jib and pole. She leaned graciously into the breeze, without her white bridge, which was made of Canadian pine, being dampened by any spray from the small waves sliced through by her stem perpendicular to the water.

The distance separating the two small Hebridean islands of Iona and Staffa is very short. With a fair wind, a yacht which could easily clear eight miles an hour without being too pushed, could have made it in twenty to twenty-five minutes. But at that moment they were heading into the wind, though it was but a slight breeze at the most. Moreover the tide was going out, and they had to tack several times against a fairly strong ebb tide before arriving at Staffa.

This was however of little consequence to Miss Campbell. The *Clorinda* had set out, that was the main thing. An hour later Iona was lost in the morning mist and with it the detested image of that spoilsport whose very name Helena wanted to forget.

And she said so frankly to her uncles: 'Am I not right papa Sam?'

'Completely right, my dear Helena.'

'Do you not approve of me, mama Sib?'

'Absolutely.'

'Shall we agree,' she added kissing them, 'that it really was not a good idea of yours to want to give me such a husband?'

And they both agreed.

In short, it was a charming trip whose only fault was that of being too short. And what prevented them from prolonging it, from allowing the yawl to run likewise before the Green Ray, and from going to look for it in the middle of the Atlantic? But no! It had been agreed that they would go to Staffa, and John Olduck had made arrangements to reach the famous Hebridean island with the beginning of the incoming tide.

At about eight o'clock, breakfast, which consisted of tea, butter and sandwiches, was served in the dining room of the *Clorinda*. The guests were in good humour, and feted the fare on board gaily without regretting that in the inn on Iona. How ungrateful they were!

When Miss Campbell went back up to the bridge, the yacht had taken a new line and changed her tack. She was then heading back towards the superb lighthouse constructed on the rock of Skerrymore, whose top-class light stands 150 feet above sea level. The breeze had picked up and the *Clorinda* was fighting against the ebb tide with its great white sails, but was gaining little on Staffa. And yet she was 'cutting the feather', to use the Scottish way of referring to the speed of her progress.

Miss Campbell was in the stern, half lying on one of those thick cushions of rough canvas that are used onboard pleasure boats of British origin. She was entranced by this rapid motion, which was like that of a skater swept along on the surface of an icy lake, and which was not disrupted by the jolts of a road or the vibrations of a railway. Nothing could have been more graceful than the elegant *Clorinda*, as, leaning slightly over the clear water, she bobbed up and down in the waves. Sometimes she seemed to glide in the air like a great bird lifted up by its powerful wings.

Miss Campbell was half lying on one of those thick cushions…

This sea, shielded by the large Hebridean islands to the north and the south, and sheltered by the coast to the east, was like an inland basin whose waters could not be disturbed by any breeze.

The yacht ran obliquely towards the isle of Staffa, a large isolated rock off the coast of the Isle of Mull, which rises up no more than 100 feet above high tides. You might have thought that it was it that was moving, sometimes showing its basalt cliffs to the west, sometimes the grim mass of its rocks on its eastern side. An optical illusion made it appear as if it was pivoting on its base, conditioned by the angle at which the *Clorinda* happened to approach or turn in succession.

However, despite the ebb tide and the breeze, the yacht advanced a little. When she veered towards the west, beyond the extreme headlands of Mull, the sea shook her more forcibly, but she held herself gallantly against the first waves of the open sea, then with the next tack, she found herself back in tranquil waters, which rocked her as a cradle does a baby.

At around eleven o'clock, the *Clorinda* had advanced far enough north to allow herself to be carried to Staffa. The sheets were slackened, the jib sail taken down from the head of the mast, and the captain made preparations to moor.

There is no port on Staffa, but it is easy to glide along the cliffs to the east under any wind, in the midst of rocks capriciously weathered by some convulsion of geological periods. All the same, in very bad weather, the place would not be suitable for a vessel above a certain tonnage.

The *Clorinda* thus ranged herself fairly close to this seam of black basalt. She manoeuvred adroitly, leaving on one side the Rock of the Bouchaille, whose bundle of prism-shaped shafts could be seen in the low sea, and on the other side the causeway that runs along the coast to the left. This is the best mooring point on the island. It is the place where the vessels, which bring the tourists, come to pick them up again after they have walked on the hills of Staffa.

The *Clorinda* entered a small cove, almost at the entrance to Clamshell Cave. Her rigging leaned forward as her halyards were loosed, her staysail was struck, and her anchor was dropped at the mooring post.

A moment later, Miss Campbell and her companions disembarked onto the first basalt steps to the left of the cave. A wooden flight of steps with a railing led from the first stratum to the rounded back of the island.

They ascended and reached the higher plateau.

They were finally on Staffa, as far out of the inhabited world as if some storm had cast them onto the most deserted of Pacific islands.

18

Staffa

ALTHOUGH STAFFA IS just a small island, at least nature has made it into the most unusual of all the Hebridean archipelago. This large oval-shaped rock, a mile long and half a mile wide, hides marvellous caves of basalt origin under its shell. It is therefore the meeting point for geologists as well as for tourists. However, neither Miss Campbell nor the Melville brothers had yet visited Staffa. Only Oliver Sinclair was aware of its delights. He was thus appointed to do the honours of this island, to which they had come to spend a few days.

This rock is entirely the result of the crystallisation of an enormous mass of basalt, which solidified there at an early stage in the formation of the earth's crust. And that dates from a long time ago. In fact, according to Hemholtz' observations – formed from Bischof's experiments on the cooling down of basalt, which can only be melted at a temperature of two thousand degrees – it would have needed no less than three hundred and fifty million years to have had time to cool down completely. It must thus have been at a fantastically remote era that the solidification of the globe, after having passed from a gaseous to a liquid state, began to take place.

Had Aristobulus Ursiclos been there, he would have had material for a fine dissertation on the phenomena of historical geology. But he was far away, Miss Campbell no longer gave him a thought, and, as brother Sam said to brother Sib: 'Leave the fly alone on the wall!'

A very Scottish phrase, which means 'Let sleeping dogs lie!'

Staffa

Then they looked around and at one another.

'First of all,' said Oliver Sinclair, 'we ought to take possession of our new home.'

'Without forgetting what we came here for', replied Miss Campbell smiling.

'Without forgetting that, I should think not!' cried Oliver Sinclair. 'Let's go and look for an observation post and see what the marine horizon is like to the west of our isle.'

'Let's go,' replied Miss Campbell, 'but the weather is a little cloudy today, and I don't think that the sunset will take place in favourable conditions.'

'We will wait, Miss Campbell, we will wait, if need be, until the bad weather of the equinox.'

'Yes, we will wait,' replied the Melville brothers, 'until Helena orders us to leave.'

'Oh, there's no rush, dear uncles', replied the young girl, who was completely happy since their departure from Iona. 'No, there's no rush, this island is charmingly situated. If you had a villa made in the middle of this meadow, which has been thrown over its surface like a green carpet, it would not be unpleasant to live here, even when the squalls, which America is so kind as to send to us, beat down on Staffa's rocks.'

'Hmm!' sniffed uncle Sib, 'they must be terrible at this extreme point of the ocean!'

'They are indeed', replied Oliver Sinclair. 'Staffa is exposed to all the winds that sweep in from the open sea, and is only sheltered on its eastern coast where the *Clorinda* is moored. The bad weather in this part of the Atlantic lasts almost nine months out of the twelve.'

'Which is why,' replied brother Sam, 'there is not a single tree to be seen. Every shred of vegetation must wither on this plateau as soon as it rises stand several feet higher than the ground.'

'Well, would not living on this island for two or three months in the summer be worth all the effort?' cried Miss Campbell. 'You should buy Staffa, uncles, if Staffa is for sale.'

Brother Sam and brother Sib had already put their hands into their pockets as if to conclude the acquisition, in their capacity as uncles who refuse none of their niece's whims.

'Who does Staffa belong to?' asked brother Sib.

'To the MacDonald family', replied Oliver Sinclair. 'They lease it for twelve pounds a year, but I don't think they would want to part with it for any price.'

'What a pity!' said Miss Campbell, who, as we well know, was very enthusiastic by nature and was then in a state of mind to be even more so.

Whilst they were talking, Staffa's new guests traversed its uneven surface, which was made up of wide green undulations. That particular day was not one of those on which the Oban steamer company visited the smaller Hebridean islands. So Miss Campbell and her party had no need to fear being bothered by tourists. They were alone on this deserted rock. A few ponies and some black cows grazed the thin grass of the plateau, which was pierced here and there by the lava flow. No shepherd had been appointed to watch them; if the small flock of four-legged islanders was observed at all, it was from afar – perhaps from Iona, or even from the coast of Mull, fifteen miles to the east.

There were no dwellings either. Only the remains of a cottage, destroyed by the terrible storms that rage between the September and March equinoxes. To tell the truth, twelve pounds is a good rent for several acres of field, whose grass is as short as old threadbare velvet.

Their exploration of the island's surface was soon complete, and nothing remained but to watch the horizon.

It was evident that they could expect nothing from the sunset that evening. With the mobility that characterises September, the sky, which had been so pure the day before, was covered over with clouds yet again. At around six o'clock, a few red clouds, the kind that announce future unrest in the atmosphere, veiled the west. The Melville brothers were even able to confirm reluctantly that the *Clorinda*'s barometer was moving back towards variable, and looked as though it would pass it.

Thus, after the sun had disappeared beneath a line that was

This cave is easy to access.

perforated by the woolly clouds over the open ocean, they all returned to the steamer. They spent the night tranquilly in the small cove, formed by the entrance to Clamshell.

The next day, 7 September, they decided to make a more complete tour of the island. Having exploring its top section, it was time to explore those underneath. Did they not need to occupy their time, since a real piece of bad luck – attributable to Aristobulus Ursiclos alone – had as yet prevented them from observing the phenomenon? Moreover, there was no reason to regret this excursion to the caves that have made this small island in the Hebridean archipelago famous.

That day was spent first of all in exploring Clamshell Cave, before which the yacht was moored. The ship's cook, acting on the instructions of Oliver Sinclair, was even to serve their midday meal there. In the cave, the guests would be able to imagine themselves shut up in the hold of a ship. In fact the prisms, which range from 40 to 50 feet in length and form the frame of the vault, resemble the timbers inside a vessel.

This cave, which is around 30 feet high, 15 feet wide and 100 feet deep, is easy to access. It opens towards the east, is sheltered from bad winds, and is not visited by the formidable waves that are launched by storms into the other caves on the island. But perhaps too, it is less interesting.

Nevertheless, the arrangement of its basalt curves, which appears to suggest the work of man rather than that of nature, is designed to astound.

Miss Campbell was enchanted by the visit. Oliver Sinclair had her admire the beauties of Clamshell, no doubt with less scientific hotchpotch than Aristobulus Ursiclos would have done, but with more artistic feeling.

'I would like a souvenir of our visit to Clamshell', said Miss Campbell.

'Nothing could be easier', replied Oliver Sinclair.

And, with a few pencil strokes, he made a rough sketch of the cave, taken from the rock that emerges at the end of the large basalt causeway. The opening of the cave, which looks like an enormous marine mammal reduced to the skeleton formed by its walls, the light flight of steps leading up to the summit of the island, and the clear and tranquil water at its entrance, under which its enormous basalt substructure is visible, were all artistically depicted on the page in the album.

At the bottom, the artist added this note, which did not spoil it:

Oliver Sinclair to Miss Campbell
Staffa, 7 September 1881

Once they had finished lunch, captain John Olduck had the largest of the *Clorinda*'s two ship's boats made ready, the passengers took their seats in it, and they headed around the island's picturesque coast to Boat Cave, which is so called because its entire inside is filled with water and it is impossible to visit it without getting your feet wet.

This cave is situated on the south-west side of the island. If there is a strong swell, it would be imprudent to enter it, for the water there is very rough and violent. But that day, although the sky was very menacing, the wind had not yet picked up, and it would not be dangerous to explore.

Just as the *Clorinda*'s boat arrived at the opening of the deep cave, the steamer, full of tourists from Oban, moored in view of the island. Very luckily, this two hour stay, during which Staffa belonged to the visitors of the *Pioneer*, would not distrurb Miss Campbell and her party. They remained unnoticed in Boat Cave during the statutory walk, which only takes in Fingal's Cave and the heights of Staffa. There was thus no occasion for them to come into contact with this somewhat noisy group of people – which they were glad about and with just cause. For might not Aristobulus Ursiclos have taken the steamer, which had just called at Iona, after the sudden disappearance of his companions, in order to return to Oban? That, above all others, was a meeting to be avoided.

Whether that ousted suitor was amongst the tourists on the 7 September or not, no-one remained behind when the steamer departed. When Miss Campbell, the Melville brothers and Oliver

They remained unnoticed…

Sinclair came out of the long passageway, a sort of tunnel without an exit, which seems to have been borne into a basalt mine, they found Staffa its ordinary peaceful self, isolated on the edge of the Atlantic.

A fair number of famous caves can be cited in many places on the globe, but particularly in volcanic regions. They are distinguished by their origin, which is neptunian or plutonic.

Of these cavities, some have been hollowed by the water, which bites into and wears away even granite masses little by little, to the point at which they become vast caves, like the caves at Crozon in Brittany, those of Bonifacio in Corsica, of Morghatten in Norway, St Michael's Cave in Gibraltar, at Scratchell on the coast of the Isle of Wight, and those of Tourane in the marble cliffs off the Cochinchine coast.

Others are formed very differently by the retreat of granite or basalt walls, produced by the cooling off of igneous rocks, and, in their structure, they have a brutal character that is absent from the Neptunian caves.

For the first, nature, faithful to her principles, has economised on effort; for the second, she has economised on time. The famous Fingal's Cave belongs to that group whose matter has bubbled in the fires of geological eras.

The next day was to be devoted to the exploration of this wonder of the earth's crust.

19

Fingal's Cave

HAD THE *CLORINDA*'s captain been in any of the United Kingdom's ports in the last twenty-four hours, he would have been aware of a less than reassuring weather forecast for ships in the process of crossing the Atlantic.

A squall had been announced by telegram from New York. After having crossed the ocean from west to north-east, it was now threatening to launch itself brutally at the coasts of Ireland and Scotland before dying out beyond the Norwegian coast.

But, in default of this telegram, the yacht's barometer indicated large atmospheric disturbances in the near future, which a prudent sailor had to take notice of.

Thus, on the morning of the 8 September, John Oldbuck, somewhat worried, made his way to the most westerly of Staffa's rocks in order to check on the state of the sky and the sea.

Some innocuous looking clouds, wisps of haze rather than true cloud, were already racing along at a great speed. The breeze was increasing, and, before long, would turn into a gale. The sea was flecked with white horses in the distance; waves were breaking with a crash against the basalt piles that stand up like spikes at the foot of the island.

John Olduck did not feel at ease. Although the *Clorinda* was relatively sheltered in Clamshell Cove, it was not a secure mooring site, even for a fairly small boat. The power of the water sweeping in between the islets and the eastern causeway would produce a formidable backwash that would render the yacht's situation dangerous. It was thus necessary to take action, and to take it before the pass became impracticable.

When the captain was back on board, he found his passengers and made them aware of his apprehensions and of the necessity, as he saw it, of getting underway as soon as possible. Should they delay for several hours, they would run the risk of finding a raging sea in the 15 mile strait separating Staffa and the Isle of Mull. Now, it was behind this island that he wanted to take refuge, and more particularly at the small port of Achnacraig, where the *Clorinda* would have nothing to fear from the wind off the open sea.

'Leave Staffa!' cried Miss Campbell first of all. 'And lose such a magnificent horizon!'

'I believe that it would be extremely dangerous to remain moored in Clamshell', replied John Oldbuck.

'If it is necessary, my dear Helena', said brother Sam.

'Yes, if it is necessary!' added brother Sib.

Oliver Sinclair, seeing the displeasure that this hasty departure caused Miss Campbell, said quickly, 'How long do you think that this storm will last, Captain Olduck?'

'Two or three days at the most at this time of the year', the Captain replied.

'And you believe it is necessary to leave?'

'Necessary and urgent.'

'What do you plan to do?'

'Set off this very morning. With the wind that has picked up, we could be in Achnacraig before the evening, and we will return to Staffa as soon as the bad weather passes.'

'Why not return to Iona? The *Clorinda* could be there in an hour', asked brother Sam.

'No, no, not Iona!' said Miss Campbell, before whom the shadow of Aristobulus Ursiclos loomed.

'We would not be much safer in Iona than we are moored in Staffa', remarked John Olduck.

'Well,' said Oliver Sinclair, 'leave captain, leave immediately for Achnacraig and leave us on Staffa.'

'On Staffa!' replied John Olduck. 'There's not even a house to shelter you!'

'Might not Clamshell Cave suffice as a house for a few days?' resumed Oliver Sinclair. 'What will we want for? Nothing! We have enough provisions on board, the bedding from our bunks, a change of clothes, all of which can be got off board, and finally a cook who would ask nothing better than to stay with us!'

'Yes! Yes!' replied Miss Campbell, clapping her hands. 'Leave Captain, leave immediately with your yacht for Achnacraig and leave us on Staffa. We will be like people abandoned on a desert island. We will willingly lead a shipwrecked existence. We will watch out for the return of the *Clorinda* with the emotions, the agony and the worry of the Robinsons when they saw a ship off the coast of their island. What did we come here for? Romance wasn't it, Mr Sinclair? And what could be more romantic than this situation, uncles? And, moreover, a storm and gale on this poetic island, the anger of a hyperborean sea, the ossianesque battle of the unleashed elements! I would regret it all my life if I missed this sublime spectacle! So leave, Captain Olduck! We will stay here and wait for you.'

'But...' said the Melville brothers, who uttered this timid word almost simultaneously.

'I believe my uncles have spoken their mind,' replied Miss Campbell, 'but I think I know the way to bring them around to my opinion.'

And she went up to each of them and gave them their morning kiss.

'One for you, Uncle Sam. One for you, Uncle Sib. I expect you don't have anything to say now.'

They didn't even think of making the least objection. Since their niece wanted to remain on Staffa, why not remain on Staffa. How was it they hadn't come up with such a simple and natural idea that would be in all their interests?

But the idea had come from Oliver Sinclair, and Miss Campbell thought fit to thank him for it particularly.

With everything decided, the sailors carried off all the objects that were needed for their stay on the island. Clamshell was quickly transformed into a make-shift residence called Melville House. They would be just as comfortable there, perhaps even more comfortable, than in the inn on Iona. The cook took charge of finding a suitable place for his operations at the entrance to the cave, in a crevice that had evidently been designed for that use.

Then Miss Campbell and Oliver Sinclair, the Melville brothers, dame Bess and Partridge left the *Clorinda,* but only after John Olduck had left the yacht's small dinghy at their disposal, which could prove useful for them for travelling from one rock to the next.

An hour later the *Clorinda*, with reefed sails, her pole mast housed and bad weather jib set, cast off so as to skirt around the north of Mull to reach Achnacraig through the strait that separates the island from the mainland. Her passengers, high up on Staffa, followed her with their eyes as far as they could. Bending to the breeze, like a seagull whose wings graze the waves, half an hour later she disappeared behind the isle of Gometra.

But although the weather was threatening, the sky was not cloudy. The sun still shone through the large gaps in the clouds, which the wind half-opened at its zenith. They were able to walk on the island and skirt around it following the foot of the basalt cliffs. So the first care of Miss Campbell and the Melville brothers, under the guidance of Oliver Sinclair, was to visit Fingal's Cave.

Tourists who come from Iona usually visit this large cave using the small boats from the Oban steamer. But it is possible to get right to the back by landing on the rocks to the right where there is a sort of practicable quay.

This was how Oliver Sinclair had decided to explore the cave without using the *Clorinda's* dinghy.

They thus left Clamshell and took the causeway that runs along the edge of the coast on the eastern side of the island. The tops of the shafts, driven in vertically as if some engineer had built basalt piles there, formed a solid and dry pavement at the foot of the large rocks. During the walk, which took several minutes, they talked and admired the islands caressed by the backwash, the bases of which could be seen through the green sea.

It is impossible to imagine a more spectacular route to take to this cave, which was in itself worthy of being inhabited by some hero from *One Thousand and One Nights*.

When they arrived at the south-western side of the island, Oliver Sinclair had his companions climb some natural steps, which would not have been out of place on the staircase of a palace.

It is at the corner of the landing stage that the external pillars rise up, grouped against the walls of the cave like those in the small temple of Vesta in Rome, but placed side by side in a way that concealed the main structure. On their summit is supported the enormous mass of rocks which forms this corner of the island. The oblique cleavage of these rocks, which seem to be arranged in the pattern of those geometrically cut stones that form the intrados of a vault, contrasts singularly with the vertical form of the columns that support it.

At the foot of the steps, the sea, less calm, already stirred by the disturbance in the open ocean, rose and fell softly as if breathing. The entire bedrock of the cliff was reflected in it, its black shadow undulating on the water.

When they arrived at the higher landing stage, Oliver Sinclair turned to the left and showed Miss Campbell a sort of straight quay, or rather a natural path, which follows the wall to the back of the cave. A handrail, composed of iron uprights embedded into the basalt, ran between the wall and the steep edge of the small quay.

'Oh', said Miss Campbell, 'this handrail spoils the palace of Fingal for me somewhat!'

'Indeed,' said Oliver Sinclair, 'it is the intervention of man's hand in nature's work.'

'If it is useful, we should make use of it', said brother Sam.

'And I am going to!' added brother Sib.

The visitors stopped upon entering Fingal's Cave upon the advice of their guide.

A sort of nave opened up before them, high and deep, full of a mysterious shadowy light. The gap between the two lateral walls, at sea level, measured around 34 feet. To the right and left, basalt pillars, pressed against one another, hid, as in certain cathedrals from the late Gothic period, the mass of the supporting walls. At the head of the pillars sprung an enormous pointed vault, which, at its keystone, rose 50 feet above the average watermark.

Miss Campbell and her companions, filled with wonder at this first view, were finally forced to drag themselves away from their contemplation and to follow the projection which forms the internal path.

There, ranged in perfect order, stood hundreds of prismatic columns, unequal in size, similar to the products of a gigantic crystallisation process. Their fine sides stand out as clearly as if the chisel of a sculptor had filed their lines. The exterior angles of the one adapted themselves geometrically to the interior angles of another. There were three sides to some, four sides to others, a few with five or six, even seven or eight – which gave a variety to the general uniformity of the style, proving that nature has an artistic sense.

The light coming in from outside played upon all the different facets. Falling on the water inside, reflected as in a mirror, covering the submarine stones and aquatic plants with green tints, or shades of sombre red or clear yellow, it illuminated the basalt projections, which formed an irregular ceiling to the vault of this hypogeum, unrivalled throughout the world, with a thousand rays.

Within, a sort of sonorous silence reigned – if these two words can be connected – this silence peculiar to deep caves, which visitors do not dream of interrupting. Only the wind carried its long chords into the cave. They seemed to be made from a melancholic series of reduced sevenths, rising and falling little by little. Under its powerful whistle, it almost seemed as if the prisms were resonating like the reeds of an enormous harmonica. Was not this bizarre effect the origin of the name 'An-Na-Vine' or the harmonious grotto, as the cave is called in the Celtic language?

'What name could be better suited to it?' said Oliver Sinclair, 'For Fingal was Ossian's father, and Ossian's genius united poetry and music in a single art.'

'Undoubtedly,' replied brother Sam, 'but as Ossian himself said: "When now shall I hear the bard? When rejoice at the fame of my

Beyond, the horizon, where the sky and water met…

fathers? The harp is not strung on Morven. The voice of music ascends not on Cona."

'Yes', added brother Sib, 'Dead, with the mighty, is the bard. Fame is in the desert no more.'

The total depth of this cave is estimated to be around 500 feet. At the back of the nave appears a sort of organ-case, where there are a number of columns smaller than those at the entrance, but equally perfect in form.

There Oliver Sinclair, Miss Campbell and her uncles decided to stop for a moment. From this point, the perspective of the open sky is spectacular. The sea, impregnated with light, allows the structure of the submarine depths to be seen, formed from the ends of the shafts, which have between four and seven sides, fitting together exactly like the squares of a mosaic. On the lateral walls, an astonishing play of light and shadow took place. All was extinguished when some cloud fell before the opening of the cave, like a gauze curtain before the stage of a theatre. On the contrary, all was resplendent and gay with the seven colours of the prism, whenever a beam of sunlight, refracted by the crystal depths, shot up in long lines of light right up to the roof of the nave.

Outside the sea broke on the first stratums of the gigantic arch. This frame, as black as ebony, owed its entire worth to the background. Beyond, the horizon, where the sky and water met, appeared in all its splendour, with Iona lying two miles distant in the open sea, the ruins of its monastery standing out in white.

All stood in ecstasy before this fairy-like scene, unable to put their impressions into words.

'What an enchanted palace!' Miss Campbell said finally, 'It would be a very prosaic mind that refuses to believe that a God created it for the sylphs and mermaids. Who else do the sounds of this vast Aeolian harp vibrate for, when the wind blows? Is it not this supernatural music that Waverly heard in his dreams, this voice of Selma whose chords our novelist noted to rock his heroes in?'

'You are right Miss Campbell,' replied Oliver, 'and no doubt when Walter Scott was searching for images in the poetic past of the Highlands, he thought of Fingal's palace.'

'I would like to call up the spirit of Ossian here!' resumed the enthusiastic young girl. 'Why should the invisible bard not reappear at my voice after fifteen centuries of slumber? I like to think that the ill-fated one, blind like Homer and a poet like him, singing of the great deeds of his time, has more than once taken refuge in this palace, which still bears the name of his father! There doubtless, the echoes of Fingal have often repeated his epic and lyrical inspirations in the purest Gaelic accent and idioms. Do you not think, Mr Sinclair, that the aged Ossian might have sat himself in the very place where we are, and that the sounds of his harp must have mingled with the hoarse accents of Selma's voice?'

'How could I not believe in what you say with such a tone of conviction, Miss Campbell?' said Oliver Sinclair.

'Shall I call him?' murmured Miss Campbell.

And in a clear voice, she called out the name of the ancient bard several times through the vibrations of the wind.

But, however much Miss Campbell wished for it, and although she called three times, only the echo replied. Ossian's spirit failed to appear in the paternal palace.

Meanwhile, the sun had disappeared under a thick mist, the cave was filling with heavy shadows, and the sea was beginning to swell outside, its long undulations were already breaking noisily against the base of the rocks.

The visitors made their way back along the narrow path, half covered with the spray from the waves; they turned the corner of the island and were buffeted by the wind from the open sea. They then found themselves for a short while sheltered on the causeway.

The bad weather had increased markedly in the last two hours. The squall was gaining strength, throwing itself against the Scottish coast, and was threatening to turn into a storm.

But Miss Campbell and her companions, protected by the basalt cliffs, were easily able to reach Clamshell.

The next day, the barometer fell again, and the wind raged impetuously. The clouds were thicker and more livid, filling the sky and hanging low over the ground. It still did not rain, but the sun no longer shone, except at rare intervals.

Miss Campbell did not appear as exasperated by this bad weather as might have been expected. This mode of existence on a deserted island, lashed by the storm, satisfied her ardent nature. Like one of Walter Scott's heroines, she loved to wander amongst the rocks of Staffa, absorbed in new thoughts, usually alone, everyone respecting her solitude.

Several times she returned to Fingal's Cave, whose poetic odd-ness attracted her. She spent whole hours in a day dream there, and took little notice of the recommendations of others not to wander there imprudently.

The next day, 9 September, the Scottish coast bore the brunt of the storm. In the centre of the squall, aerial currents moved with unequalled violence. It was a storm. It would have been impossi-ble for anything to resist it up on the island's plateau.

At around seven in the evening, with dinner awaiting them in Clamshell Cave, Oliver Sinclair and the Melville brothers had reason to be extremely worried.

Miss Campbell had left at three without saying where she was going, and had not yet returned.

They waited patiently, though with growing anxiety, until six o'clock. Miss Campbell did not return.

Oliver Sinclair went up onto the island's plateau several times, but without seeing anyone.

The storm then unleashed itself with unparalleled fury and the sea, stirred up in enormous waves, crashed against the part of the island that was exposed to the south-west without mercy.

'Poor Miss Campbell!' Oliver Sinclair cried suddenly. 'If she is still in Fingal's Cave, we must get her out or she is lost!'

20

For Miss Campbell

A FEW MOMENTS LATER, Oliver Sinclair, having run quickly along the causeway, arrived in front of the entrance to the cave, near to where the basalt steps rose.

The Melville brothers and Partridge had followed close behind him.

Dame Bess had remained in Clamshell, waiting with inexpressible anxiety, preparing everything to receive Helena on her return.

The sea had already risen to such a level as to cover the higher landing. It was flooding over the handrail, making it impossible to enter the cave by the path.

The fact that it was impossible to enter the cave meant that it was also impossible to leave it. If Miss Campbell was inside, she was imprisoned there! But how could they tell? How could they reach her?

'Helena! Helena!'

Could this name ever be heard, thrown in as it was amongst the roaring of the waves? It was as if a thunder of wind and waves was surging into the cave. Neither voice nor sight would be powerful enough to penetrate it.

'Perhaps Miss Campbell isn't there?' said brother Sam, clinging to this hope.

'Where is she then?' replied brother Sib.

'Yes! Where is she then?' cried Oliver Sinclair. 'Have I not searched for her in vain on the island's plateau, and in the midst of the rocks on the coast, everywhere? Would she not already have returned to us if she could return? She is there... there!'

And they recalled the enthusiastic and reckless desire that the imprudent young girl had several times expressed of being present in Fingal's Cave during a storm. Had she then forgotten that the sea, whipped up by the storm, would rush right to its back and turn it into a prison, whose door it was impossible to force open?

What could they do now to reach her, and to save her?

Under the impetus of the storm, which whipped this corner of the island without mercy, the waves sometimes reached almost to the top of the vault. There they broke with a deafening crash. The excess water, pushed back on impact, fell back in foaming streams, like the cataracts of a Niagara. But the lower portion of the waves, pushed by the swell of the open ocean, rushed right to the back of the cave with the violence of a torrent whose gate has suddenly broken. It was thus the very back of the cave that the sea collided with.

In what place might Miss Campbell have found a refuge that was not assailed by these waves? The chevet of the cave was directly exposed to their blows, and, in both their ebb and flow, they must have swept the path with irresistible force.

And yet they still refused to believe that the reckless young girl was there! How could she have resisted the furious sea's invasion into this impasse? Would not her body have been torn to pieces, and her mutilated corpse taken up by the waves and carried outside? Would not then the current of the rising tide have dragged it along the causeway and the reefs to Clamshell?

'Helena! Helena!'

The name was obstinately shouted again and again through the hubbub of wind and waves.

There was no shout of reply, and nor could there have been.

'No! No! She isn't in the cave!' repeated the Melville brothers in despair.

'She is there!' said Oliver Sinclair.

And with one hand he pointed to a piece of cloth, which a retreating wave had thrown onto one of the basalt steps.

Oliver Sinclair rushed at the scrap.

It was the snod or Scottish ribbon that Miss Campbell wore in her hair.

'Helena! Helena!'

Was it possible to be in doubt any longer?

But if this ribbon had been torn from her, might it not be that Miss Campbell had been crushed by the same blow against the walls of Fingal's Cave?

'I will find out!' cried Oliver Sinclair.

And taking advantage of the retreat of the waves, which left the path half clear, he seized the first of the handrails uprights, but a mass of water tore him off and threw him back onto the landing.

Had Partridge not, at the risk of his life, thrown himself onto him, Oliver Sinclair would have rolled down to the last step and been dragged away by the sea without anyone having been able to rescue him.

Oliver Sinclair had stood back up. His resolve to enter the cave had not been weakened.

'Miss Campbell is there!' he repeated. 'She is alive because her body has not been swept out like this scrap of cloth! So it is possible that she has found refuge in some crevice! But her strength will be used up quickly! She won't be able to hold out until the sea has gone down... so we must get to her!'

'I'll go!' said Partridge.

'No! I will!' replied Oliver Sinclair.

He was going to make one last attempt to get to Miss Campbell, and yet the odds of it succeeding were barely one in a hundred.

'Wait for us here, sirs', he said to the Melville brothers. 'We will return in five minutes. Come Partridge!'

The two uncles remained at the outer corner of the island, in the shelter of the cliff where the sea could not reach them, whilst Oliver Sinclair and Partridge returned to Clamshell as quickly as possible.

It was half past eight in the evening.

Five minutes later the young man and the old servant reappeared, dragging along the causeway the *Clorinda*'s small dinghy, which Captain John Olduck had left them.

Was Oliver Sinclair going to throw himself into the cave by sea, since the passage by land was forbidden him?

Within the space of a second…

Yes! He was going to attempt it. It was his life he was risking. He knew it and yet he didn't hesitate.

The dinghy was brought to the foot of the steps, sheltered from the surf by one of the basalt steps.

'I'll go with you', said Partridge.

'No Partridge,' Oliver Sinclair replied, 'No! We cannot over-burden such a small vessel for no good reason! If Miss Campbell is still alive, I will suffer alone!'

'Oliver!' shouted the two brothers, who couldn't hold back their tears, 'Oliver, save our girl!'

The young man grasped them by the hand, then he jumped into the dinghy, sat down on the bench in the middle, grasped the oars, headed straight off into the eddy and waited for an instant for the ebb of an enormous wave, which took him opposite Fingal's Cave.

There the dinghy was lifted up, but Oliver Sinclair, with a deft manoeuvre, succeeded in keeping it straight. If he had been caught amidships, he would inevitably have capsized.

For the first time the sea lifted the frail craft almost to the height of the vault. You might well have thought that the shell would break against the rocky mass, but the wave retreated and carried it back out to the open sea with a backward movement that it was impossible to resist.

The craft was tossed thus three times, first precipitated towards the cave, then thrust backwards without having found a passage through the waters, which barred the opening. Oliver Sinclair retained his self-control and kept himself stable with his oars.

Finally, a larger crest raised the dinghy; it swayed for a moment on this liquid back, almost to the height of the island's plateau, and then a deep trough opened to the foot of the cave and Oliver Sinclair was launched downwards obliquely, as if he had descended the slopes of a cataract.

A cry of terror escaped the witnesses to this scene. It seemed that the craft would inevitably be dashed against the left-hand pillars at the corner of the entrance.

But the intrepid young man righted his dinghy with the stroke of an oar. The opening was then gained, and, with the rapidity of an arrow, he disappeared into the entrance of the cave, a little before the sea rose again in an enormous mass.

A second later the sheets of liquid came down like an avalanche, breaking against the higher ridge of the island.

Would the dinghy be dashed against the far end, and would there be two victims instead of one?

But there were none. Oliver Sinclair had travelled quickly without hitting the uneven roof of the vault. By leaning back flat in the craft, he was spared the impact of the basalt stacks which projected out. Within the space of a second, he had reached the opposite wall, his only fear being that he would be pushed out with the backwash before he was able to grab hold of some projection at the back.

Luckily the dinghy, in a blow softened by the ebb of the waves, bumped into the pillars of that organ case erected in the chevet of Fingal's Cave. It broke in half, but Oliver Sinclair was able to catch hold of a piece of basalt. He clung to it with the tenacity of a drowning man, and then heaved himself up to a place where he was sheltered from the sea.

A moment later, the shattered dinghy, which had been caught by a retreating wave, was thrown out of the cave, and the Melville brothers and Partridge saw the wreck reappear and thought that the brave rescuer must have perished.

21

A Storm in a Cave

OLIVER SINCLAIR WAS unhurt and, for the moment, safe. The darkness was then so profound that he could see nothing inside. The dusky daylight only penetrated in the intervals between waves, when the entrance was half free from the mass of water.

But Oliver Sinclair tried to make out where Miss Campbell could have found a refuge... in vain.

He called: 'Miss Campbell! Miss Campbell!'

It is almost impossible to describe what he felt when he heard a voice reply: 'Mr Oliver! Mr Oliver!'

Miss Campbell was alive.

But where could she have taken refuge out of the reach of the waves' assault?

Oliver Sinclair crawled along the path skirting around the back of Fingal's Cave.

In the wall on the left was a basalt hiding hole, formed by a crevice hollowed out like a niche. The pillars there were disjointed. The recess had quite a large opening, but became narrower, so as to leave space only for one person. Legend gave this hole the name of 'Fingal's Chair'.

It was in this recess that Miss Campbell had taken refuge when she had been surprised by the invasion of the sea.

Some hours before, with the tide going out, the entrance to the cave had been easily practicable, and the imprudent young woman had made her daily visit. There, plunged in her dreams, she was unaware of the danger posed by the rising tide, and had seen nothing of what was happening outside. Imagine her horror when she tried to leave and found that there was no longer a way through this invading water.

However, Miss Campbell did not lose her head. She searched for some place to take shelter, and, after two or three vain attempts to regain the landing outside, she was able to reach Fingal's Chair, though not without the risk of being swept away twenty times.

It is there that Oliver Sinclair found her curled up, out of the reach of the blows from the sea.

'Ah, Miss Campbell!' he cried. 'How could you have been so reckless as to expose yourself in such a manner at the beginning of a storm! We thought you were lost!'

'And you came to save me, Mr Sinclair', replied Miss Campbell, who was more touched by the young man's courage than she was scared by the dangers that she might still have to face!

'I came to rescue you from a perilous situation, Miss Campbell, and with God's help I will succeed!'

'Are you not afraid?'

'I'm not afraid... no! Since you are here, I no longer fear anything... And moreover, how could I feel anything other than admiration at such a spectacle? Look!'

Miss Campbell had recoiled to the back of the recess. Oliver Sinclair stood in front of her, trying to shelter her as best he could whenever some particularly furious wave threatened to reach her.

They were both silent. Did Oliver Sinclair need to say anything to make himself understood? What was the use of words for expressing all that Miss Campbell felt?

Meanwhile, the young man watched the threat from outside growing with indescribable anxiety, not for himself but for Miss Campbell. Did he not know that the storm was being unleashed with increasing fury from the sound of the wind howling and the din of the sea? Did he not notice the level of the sea rising, and know that the tide would swell it for several hours yet?

Where would the water stop rising? The swell in the open ocean would make its level abnormally high. He could not tell, but what was only too visible was that the cave was filling little by little. If the darkness there was not yet complete, it was

'Oliver! Oliver!' shouted Miss Campbell...

because the crests of the waves was confusedly impregnated by the light outside. Moreover, large phosphorescent patches threw out a sort of electric fire here and there, which clung to the corners of the basalt and lit up the groins of the prisms, leaving behind a vague and livid light.

During these quick flashes, Oliver Sinclair turned towards Miss Campbell. He looked at her with an emotion that was not caused by the danger alone.

Miss Campbell was smiling at the sublime nature of the spectacle – a storm in this cave!

At that moment, a heavy swell rose to the crevice of Fingal's Chair. Oliver Sinclair thought that they would both be dislodged from their shelter.

He seized the young girl in his arms as if she was prey that the sea wanted to snatch from him.

'Oliver! Oliver!' shouted Miss Campbell, with a movement of terror during which she was no longer mistress of herself.

'Fear nothing Helena!' replied Oliver Sinclair. 'I will defend you, Helena! I...'

He said that. He would defend her! But how? How would he be able to shield her from the violence of the waves if their fury grew, if the waters rose yet higher and the place at the back of the recess became untenable? Where else could he find a refuge? Where would he find a shelter that was out of the reach of this monstrous uprising of the sea? All these eventualities appeared to him in their terrible reality.

Self-possession was everything. Oliver Sinclair resolved to retain his composure.

And it was necessary, and all the more so since physical, if not emotional, strength was beginning to elude the young girl. Exhausted by a struggle which had lasted too long, she was beginning to react. Oliver Sinclair felt that she was already weakening little by little. He wanted to reassure her, even though he felt hope abandoning himself.

'Helena... my dear Helena!' he murmured. 'When I got back to Oban I found out... it was you... it was thanks to you that I was saved from the Gulf of Corryvreckan!'

'Oliver... you knew...!' replied Miss Campbell in a tiny voice.

'Yes... and I will acquit myself today... I will save you from Fingal's Cave!'

How could Oliver Sinclair dare to talk of salvation at that moment, when the mass of water was breaking at the foot of the recess! He succeeded only in part in defending his companion from their attacks. Two or three times he was almost dragged away... And if he did resist, it was only by a superhuman effort, feeling the arms of Miss Campbell almost knotted around his waist, and knowing that the sea would have carried her away with him.

It must have been about half past nine in the evening. The storm must have reached its maximum intensity then. In fact, the rising water hurled itself into Fingal's Cave with the intensity of an avalanche. There was a deafening crash when it hit the back and the lateral walls, and such was its fury that pieces of basalt became detached from the walls and made black holes in the phosphorescent foam as they fell.

Under this assault, the violence of which nothing could withstand, would the pillars cave in stone by stone? Was the vault at risk of collapsing? Oliver Sinclair feared it all. He also felt himself overcome by an insurmountable torpor, against which he tried to react. Sometimes there was not enough air. Though it came in abundantly with the waves, they seemed to draw it all out again when they retreated.

In these conditions, Miss Campbell, who was exhausted and whose strength was leaving her, was overcome by faintness.

'Oliver... Oliver...' she murmured and fell into his arms.

Oliver Sinclair had huddled up with the young girl in the deepest part of the recess. She felt cold and lifeless. He wanted to warm her and transfer all the heat that remained within him to her. But already the water was halfway up his body and, if he in turn lost consciousness, they were both lost!

However, the intrepid young man had the strength to resist for several more hours. He supported Miss Campbell and covered her from the impact of the sea's blows; he counteracted them by

He began to follow the narrow ledge.

leaning into the basalt projections. And all in the midst of an obscurity that the extinction of the phosphorescence had made profound, in the midst of this continuous thunder of collisions, roaring and whistles. It was no longer the voice of Selma resounding in Fingal's palace! It was the terrible barking of the dogs of Kamchatka, which, Michelet says, 'roam about in bands of thousands during the long nights, howling furiously at the roaring of the North Sea!'

Finally the tide began to go out. Oliver Sinclair was able to make out that the swell in the open sea had died down a little as the water level went down. The darkness was then so complete that outside it was relatively light. In this semi-darkness, the opening of the cave, which was no longer obstructed by the rolling of the sea, was only a confused outline. Soon only the spray reached the seat of Fingal's Chair. Now it was no longer that strangling lasso of waves, holding tight and tearing down. Hope returned to the heart of Oliver Sinclair.

By calculating the time that had passed since high tide, he knew that it must be after midnight. Another two hours and the path would no longer be swept by the breaking waves. It would then become practicable again. It was this that he had to attempt to see in the darkness, and it is what finally happened.

The moment had come to leave the cave.

However, Miss Campbell had not regained consciousness. Oliver Sinclair took her inert body in his arms, and slid out of Fingal's Chair. He then began to follow the narrow ledge, whose iron railings the sea's blows had twisted, uprooted and broken.

Whenever a wave reached him, he stopped for a moment or took a step back.

Finally, just as Oliver Sinclair was about to reach the outer corner, one last rush of water covered him completely... He thought that Miss Campbell and he were going to be crushed against the wall or precipitated into the rushing gulf beneath their feet...

With one last effort he managed to resist and, taking advantage of the sea's ebb, he rushed out of the cave.

In a moment he had reached the corner of the cliff where the Melville brothers, Partridge and dame Bess, who had joined them, had remained all night.

They were saved.

There this paroxysm of physical and mental energy, at which Oliver Sinclair had arrived, abandoned him in turn. After giving Miss Campbell over to the arms of dame Bess, he fell at the foot of the rocks, and lay without moving.

Without his devotion and courage, Helena would not have left Fingal's Cave alive.

22

The Green Ray

A FEW MINUTES LATER, in the fresh air at the back of Clamshell, Miss Campbell regained consciousness, as if from a dream in which the image of Oliver Sinclair had filled all the phases. She didn't even remember the dangers that her imprudence had exposed her to.

She could not yet speak, but at the sight of Oliver Sinclair, several tears of recognition came to her eyes, and she held out a hand to her saviour.

Brother Sam and brother Sib, unable to speak, embraced the young man in the same grip. Dame Bess made him curtsey after curtsey, and Partridge wanted to hug him.

Then, fatigue overcoming them, after each had changed the clothes that had been soaked by the water from the sea and sky, they all went to sleep and the night passed in peace.

But what they had felt was never to be wiped from the memory of the actors and witnesses who had had the legendary Fingal's Cave as a theatre.

The next day, while Miss Campbell rested on the couch that had been reserved for her at the back of Clamshell, the Melville brothers walked around, arm in arm, on the neighbouring part of the causeway. They said nothing, but did they need words to express the same thoughts? They both moved their head up and down at the same moment whenever they wanted to affirm something, and from left to right when they wanted to deny something. And what could they affirm, if not the fact that Oliver Sinclair had risked his life to save the imprudent young girl? And what did they deny? That their early plans might now be realised. In this mute conversation, many things were said that they foresaw would soon be accomplished. In their eyes, Oliver was no longer Oliver. He was no less than Amin, the most perfect hero of the Gaelic eras.

As for Oliver Sinclair, he was prey to a very natural over-excitement. A sort of delicacy made him want to be alone. He felt embarrassed in the presence of the Melville brothers, as if his presence alone might have appeared to exact the reward for his devotion.

After leaving Clamshell Cave, he walked on the plateau of Staffa.

At that moment, his thoughts involuntarily returned to Miss Campbell. He did not even remember the perils that he had faced and that he had shared of his own accord. What he did remember of the horrible night were the hours passed near Helena in the dark recess, when he had wrapped his arms around her to save her from the raging of the waves. He saw the face of the beautiful young girl again in the phosphorescent light, pale with fatigue rather than fear, rising up against the fury of the sea like the spirit of the storms! He heard her reply with a voice full of emotion, 'What, you knew?', when he had said 'I know what you did when I was about to perish in the Gulf of Corryvreckan!' He found himself once again at the back of the narrow shelter, that recess designed to lodge a cold stone statue, where two young people, in love, had suffered and fought side by side for such long hours. There, it was no longer Sinclair and Miss Campbell. They had called one another Oliver and Helena, as if, at the moment when death threatened them, they had wanted to take up a new life!

Such was the combination of the young man's most ardent thoughts while he wandered around on the plateau of Staffa. However much he wished to return to Miss Campbell, an invincible force held him back despite himself, because, in her presence, he would perhaps have spoken and he wished to remain silent.

Meanwhile, as happens sometimes after atmospheric distur-bances, brutally unleashed and brutally dispersed, the weather was splendid, the sky perfectly clear. Usually, these great sweeping gusts of wind from the southwest leave no trace behind, and lend the sky an incomparable level of transparency. The sun had passed its zenith and the horizon was not veiled by even the slightest shred of mist.

Oliver Sinclair, his head in a whirl, walked thus through this intense irradiation, which was reflected by the island plateau. He bathed in the midst of the warm fragrance, he breathed in the sea breeze, he immersed himself in this bracing atmosphere.

Suddenly a thought – a thought forgotten in the midst of those that now haunted his mind – came back to him, when he found himself faced by the horizon of the open sea.

'The Green Ray!' he cried. 'If ever a sky lent itself to our observations, it's this one! Not a cloud, no haze! And it is hardly likely that any will come after the terrible squall of yesterday, which must have sent them far off to the east. And Miss Campbell little suspects that this evening will perhaps bring about a splendid sunset! I must... I must warn her... and without delay!'

Oliver Sinclair, happy to have such a natural motive to return to Helena, went back towards Clamshell Cave.

Some moments later, he found himself back in the presence of Miss Campbell and her two uncles, who were looking at her affectionately whilst dame Bess held her hand.

'Miss Campbell,' he said, 'you are better! I can see you are... has your strength returned?'

'Yes Mr Oliver', replied Miss Campbell, starting at the sight of the young man.

'I think you would do well,' resumed Oliver Sinclair, 'to come out on the plateau and breathe in a little of this soft breeze, which has been purified by the storm. The sun is superb; it will revitalise you.'

'Mr Sinclair is right', said brother Sam.

'Completely right', added brother Sib.

'And also, if the whole truth is to be told, unless I am mistaken,' resumed Oliver Sinclair, 'I believe that the most cherished of your heart's desires will be accomplished within a few hours.'

'The most cherished of my heart's desires?' murmured Miss Campbell as if replying to herself.

'Yes, the sky is remarkably clear, and it is likely that the sun will set over a cloudless horizon!'

'Is it possible?' cried brother Sam.

'Is it possible?' repeated brother Sib.

'And I have reason to believe', added Oliver Sinclair, 'that you may see the Green Ray this very evening.'

'The Green Ray!' replied Miss Campbell.

And it seemed as if she was searching in her somewhat confused memory for what this Green Ray could be.

'Oh! It's true!' she added. 'We came here to see the Green Ray!'

'Let's go! Let's go!' said brother Sam, delighted at this opportunity of tearing the young girl out of the torpor into which she seemed to be falling. 'Let's go to the other side of the island.'

'And we will have a better appetite when we return', brother Sib added gaily.

It was five o'clock in the evening.

Under the leadership of Oliver Sinclair, the whole family, including dame Bess and Partridge, left Clamshell Cave immediately and ascended the wooden stairs to reach the edge of the higher plateau.

You should have seen the joy of the two uncles when they saw the magnificent sky through which the radiant star was slowly descending. Perhaps they were exaggerating, but never, no never, had they shown so much enthusiasm for the phenomenon. It was as if it was for their special benefit, and not for Miss Campbell's, that so much travelling had been carried out and so many hardships suffered on the journey from Helensburgh to Staffa, passing through Iona and Oban.

In fact, that evening the sunset promised to be so beautiful that the most insensible, the most pragmatic, the most prosaic of city merchants or negotiators from the Canongate would have admired the marine phenomenon that developed before their eyes.

Miss Campbell felt new life arise within her in this atmosphere full of the salty emanations distilled by a light breeze from the open ocean. Her beautiful eyes opened wide to take in their first images of the Atlantic. Her cheeks, rendered pale by fatigue, took on their rosy Scottish shade. How beautiful she was! How much charm there was in her person! Oliver Sinclair walked a little way behind, watching

The whole family ascended the stairs…

her in silence, and he, who up to then had accompanied her without embarrassment on her long walks, now found himself troubled and his heart anxious. He barely dared to look at her!

As for the Melville brothers, they were positively as radiant as the sun. They spoke to it with enthusiasm. They invited it to set over a cloudless horizon. They begged it to send them its last ray at the end of this beautiful day.

And between them, they repeated alternate verses of one of Ossian's poems:

'O thou that rollest above, round as the shield of my fathers! Whence are thy beams, O sun! thy everlasting light!'

'Thou comest forth, in thy awful beauty, and the stars hide themselves in the sky; the moon, cold and pale, sinks in the western wave; but thou thyself movest alone.'

'Who can be a companion of thy course? The oaks of the mountains fall; the mountains themselves decay with years; the ocean shrinks and grows again; the moon herself is lost in heaven; but thou art for ever the same, rejoicing in the brightness of thy course.'

'When the world is dark with tempests; when thunder rolls, and lightning flies; thou lookest in thy beauty from the clouds, and laughest at the storm.'

Thus, in this enthusiastic spirit, they made their way to the edge of the Staffa plateau that looks out over the open sea. There, they sat down on the furthest rocks, in front of a horizon whose finely traced line it seemed as if nothing would alter.

And this time there would be no Aristobulus Ursiclos to bring the sail of a craft in the way, or to make a cloud of seabirds rise between the setting sun and the isle of Staffa!

Meanwhile, the breeze fell as the evening did, and the last waves died away at the foot of the rocks. Further out in the open ocean, the sea was like a mirror, having that oily appearance that the least ripple would have been enough to disturb.

Circumstances lent themselves perfectly to the apparition of the phenomenon.

But half an hour later, Partridge pointed to the south and cried: 'Sail!'

A sail! Would it once again pass before the solar disc, just as it was disappearing under the water? In truth, it would have been more than just bad luck!

The vessel came out of the channel that separates the isle of Iona from the tip of Mull. She had the wind behind her, but moved more by the action of the rising tide than under the influence of the breeze, whose last breaths were barely enough to inflate her sails.

'It's the *Clorinda*,' said Oliver Sinclair, 'and as she is making her way to land to the east of Staffa, she will pass inside, and will not disturb our observation.'

It was indeed the *Clorinda*, which, having skirted around the Isle of Mull to the south, was coming back to moor in the cove at Clamshell.

All eyes thus returned to the western horizon.

The sun was already getting lower with the rapidity that seems to animate it when approaching the sea. A wide train of silver trembled on the surface of the water, launched by the disc, whose irradiation was still dazzling. Soon, from this nuance of old gold, which it took on while falling, it passed to a red-gold. When they closed their eyelids, red diamonds and yellow circles dazzled them like the swirling colours in a kaleidoscope. Faint wavy lines scored this comet-like tail, which the reflection traced on the surface of the water. It was like a spangled mass of glittering gems, whose brightness paled when approaching the shore.

There was no sign of any cloud, mist or haze, however tenuous, on the entire perimeter of the horizon. Nothing disturbed the distinctness of this circular line, which could not have been more finely traced by a compass on the whiteness of vellum.

They all stood still, more emotional than might be believed, watching the globe, which, moving obliquely to the horizon, was still sinking, and remained as if suspended for a moment on the abyss. Then the disc became deformed, modified by refraction, little by little; it extended to the detriment of its vertical diameter and took on the form of an Etruscan vase with bulging sides whose foot plunged into the water.

There was no longer any doubt that the phenomenon would

Neither Oliver nor Helena had seen the Green Ray.

appear. Nothing would disturb this admirable sunset! 'Nothing would appear to intercept the last of its rays!'

Soon the sun half-disappeared beneath the horizontal line. A few luminous jets, launched like golden arrows, hit the first rocks of Staffa.

Behind, the cliffs of Mull and the summit of Ben More grew red with a hint of fire.

Finally, there was only a narrow section of the upper arc showing above the surface of the sea.

'The Green Ray! The Green Ray!' cried the Melville brothers, dame Bess and Partridge in one voice. They had seen this incomparable tint of liquid jade for a quarter of a second.

Only Oliver and Helena had not seen the phenomenon, which had appeared after so many vigils in vain!

At the moment when the sun shot its last ray through space, their gazes met and they forgot themselves in the same contemplation!

But Helena had seen the black ray thrown out by the eyes of the young man, and Oliver the blue ray which escaped from the eyes of the young girl!

The sun had completely disappeared; neither Oliver nor Helena had seen the Green Ray.

23

Conclusion

THE NEXT DAY, 12 September, the *Clorinda* under the influence of a kind sea and favourable breeze, ran to the southwest of the Hebridean archipelago. Soon Staffa, Iona and the tip of Mull disappeared behind the high cliffs of the large island.

After a happy crossing, the yacht's passengers disembarked at the small port of Oban. Then they took the railway from Oban to Dalmally and from Dalmally to Glasgow, returning to the country house in Helensburgh through the most picturesque of Highland scenery.

Eighteen days later a marriage was celebrated with much ceremony in Saint George's Church in Glasgow. But it must be said that it was not that of Aristobulus Ursiclos and Miss Campbell. Although the fiancé was Oliver Sinclair, the brothers Sam and Sib showed no less satisfaction than their niece.

That this union, contracted under such circumstances, contained all the conditions of happiness, it is futile to state. The country house in Helensburgh, the house in West George Street in Glasgow, the entire world would have been insufficient to contain all the happiness that had arisen in Fingal's Cave.

But although Oliver Sinclair had not seen the phenomenon they had searched for so much on that last evening on the plateau of Staffa, he was keen to capture the memory of it in a more durable manner. Thus one day he published 'a sunset' with a very particular effect, in which people admired a sort of green ray of an extreme intensity, as if it had been painted with liquid emerald.

This painting prompted both admiration and discussion, some

claiming that it was the natural effect marvellously reproduced, others insisting that it was purely fantastic, and that nature never produced this effect.

This caused the two uncles great anger, for they had seen it and affirmed that the young painter was right.

'And what is more,' said brother Sam, 'it is better to see this Green Ray in a painting...'

'Than in nature,' replied brother Sib, 'as it is bad for the eyes to watch so many sunsets, one after the other.'

And the Melville brothers were right.

Two months later, the husband and wife and the two uncles were walking along the edge of the Clyde in front of the park of the country house, when they unexpectedly met Aristobulus Ursiclos.

The young scholar, who was following the dredging work being done on the river with interest, was heading towards the station in Helensburgh when he noticed his old companions from Oban.

To say that Aristobulus Ursiclos had suffered from being abandoned by Miss Campbell would be to misjudge him. He thus felt no embarrassment at finding himself in the presence of Mrs Sinclair.

They greeted one another. Aristobulus Ursiclos politely paid his compliments to the newly married couple.

The Melville brothers, seeing his good humour, were unable to hide how happy this union had made them.

'So happy,' said brother Sam, 'that sometimes, when I am alone, I catch myself smiling...'

'I catch myself crying', said brother Sib.

'Well, sirs', observed Aristobulus Ursiclos, 'it must be said, this is the first time you have been in disagreement. One cries, the other smiles...'

'It is exactly the same thing, Mr Ursiclos', said Oliver Sinclair.

'Exactly', said the young woman, holding out her hands to her two uncles.

'How is it the same thing?' replied Aristobulus Ursiclos with that air of superiority that suited him so well. 'No! Not at all! What is a smile? A wilful expression particular to the facial muscles, to which the phenomena of breathing are almost strangers, whilst tears...'

'Tears?' asked Mrs Sinclair.

'Are simply a mood which lubricates the eyeball, a composite of sodium chloride, lime phosphate and chlorate of soda!'

'You are right in terms of chemistry, sir,' said Oliver Sinclair, 'but only in chemistry.'

'I fail to understand the distinction', replied Aristobulus Ursiclos sourly.

And, saluting them with geometrical stiffness, he resumed his walk to the station with measured steps.

'So, that's Mr Ursiclos,' said Mrs Sinclair, 'who believes he can explain matters of the heart as he explained the Green Ray.'

'But in fact my dear Helena,' replied Oliver Sinclair, 'we haven't seen it, this ray that we so much wanted to see!'

'We saw something better!' the young woman said in a low voice. 'We saw happiness itself – which is what legend linked to observing the phenomenon! Since we have found it, my dear Oliver, let it be sufficient for us and let us leave the search for the Green Ray to those who don't know it and would like to!'

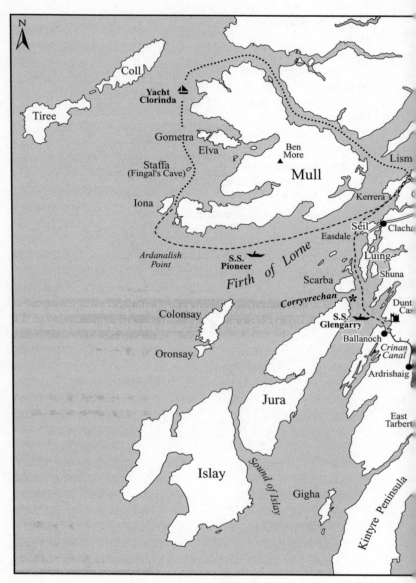

The itinerary of *The Green Ray*

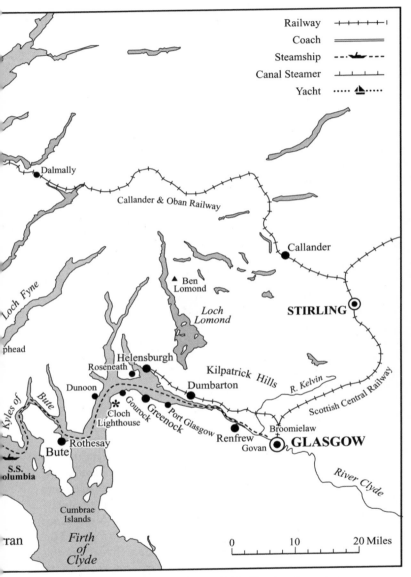

Ian Thompson, author and Mike Shand, cartographer

Afterword

LE RAYON VERT (*The Green Ray*), was first published in Paris in 1882. Of all Verne's novels, *The Green Ray* most closely follows his own travel. Verne first visited Scotland in 1859, an unknown and relatively impoverished writer. Nevertheless his wanderings in Edinburgh, Glasgow and the Trossachs provided him with the setting for *Les Indes noires* (*The Underground City*). He returned twenty years later a famous and prosperous author in his own steam yacht, the *St Michel* III, which he docked at Leith. He returned to his haunts of 1859 initially but then embarked on the classic journey which was to inspire *The Green Ray*. Miraculously the diary of this journey has survived and is conserved in France at the municipal library at Amiens. The diary is little more than notes and is rather cryptic but it allows us to trace his movements day by day and at times hour by hour. By checking timetables it is possible to reconstruct his travel in detail and to compare this with the itinerary in *The Green Ray*. The degree of accordance is remarkable, including the names of hotels that he stayed at, the names of vessels he sailed on and the specific landmarks that he remarked on as shown in the accompanying map.

The core of the story is based on the Royal Route from Glasgow to Oban, the spine of MacBrayne's network of the Clyde and the Western Isles. Leaving the Royal Hotel on Glasgow's George Square on Thursday 17 July 1879, Verne boarded the RMS *Columba* on the Broomielaw during Glasgow Fair Week. The *Columba* was the flagship, fastest and largest of MacBrayne's paddle steamers and after descending the Clyde, picking up and disembarking holiday-makers at each of the Clyde resorts, she turned north into Loch Fyne and berthed at Ardrishaig at midday. Here Verne followed the crowd across the road to the Crinan Canal where the remarkable little steamer, the *Linnet*, awaited to take the passengers the length of the canal to Crinan. At the staircase of locks at Cairnbaan, Verne followed the example of many passengers by walking along the towpath, buying milk offered by urchins, while the *Linnet* negotiated the locks. At Crinan, the PS *Chevalier* was waiting for the passengers for the onward journey to Oban. For some reason, in *The Green Ray* Verne substitutes the vessel *Glengarry*, although his diary, and press reports make it clear that the steamer concerned on that day was the *Chevalier*. Passing the Corryvreckan whirlpool, which was to be exploited to the full in the novel, Verne reached Oban at 6pm and took a room at the Caledonian Hotel on the seafront. This hotel no longer exists having been demolished and the name appropriated by the present large hotel close to the railway station.

The following morning Verne boarded the PS *Pioneer* headed for a day excursion round the Isle of Mull with stops at Iona and Staffa. At Iona the passengers were taken ashore by sturdy crofters in large rowing boats and Verne was able to visit the ruined cathedral. Back on board the *Pioneer*, the steamer headed north to Staffa and the weather being clement, again the passengers were taken ashore by rowing boat. Verne was enchanted by Fingal's Cave and there was sufficient time ashore to climb on to the plateau looking west to the Atlantic horizon. It is tempting to think that it was at this moment that Verne conceived the dramatic ending of *The Green Ray* for the novel is the story of two searches. It is the search by a young woman for true love and, to this end, the search for a meteorological phenomenon, the Green Ray. This green flash as the sun sinks below the horizon of the sea is held in folklore to guarantee that true love has been found. Both of these searches find their conclusion on the summit of Staffa. The PS *Pioneer* returned to Oban via the Sound of Mull and Verne again patronised the Caledonian Hotel before rising early the following day to take the post coach to Dalmally and thence by train to Edinburgh where he regained the *St Michel* III. Thus ended Verne's second visit to Scotland in the course of which he must have already conceived the outline of a novel which only awaited the invention of the *dramatis personae* to enact it.

The significant actors in the plot are not numerous. The most finely drawn is the heroine, Helena Campbell, an eighteen–year–old on the cusp of the transition from girl to womanhood and with a head full of romantic notions. She is an intelligent and cultured person but is also strong willed. An orphan, she is a ward of two bachelor uncles, Sam and Sib, who are anxious to find her a suitable husband without having the slightest understanding of the sentimental psychology of young women. The two men are virtual clones of each other and their speech and mannerisms are those of the generation before Helena's. They are devoted to Helena and in their anxiety to make a suitable match advance the case of an erudite but pedantic and accident prone scholar, Aristobulus Ursiclus. On hearing of this possible suitor, Helena bursts into laughter for she considers him, justifiably, as a buffoon. In any case, she has just read in a newspaper that the confirmation of true love depends on witnessing the Green Ray and hence her insistence that her uncles should take her on a mission to the Hebrides to get a clear view of the Atlantic horizon.

Finally, the handsome figure of Oliver Sinclair appears. Helena spots him in difficulty in a rowing boat caught in the Corryvreckan whirpool and insists that the Captain of the *Glengarry* should rescue him. He is a well educated young man, a member of a respected Edinburgh family and a keen marine artist. In contrast with Aristobulus, Oliver is a practical person and enthusiastically joins in the search for the Green Ray. A number of misadventures, for which Aristobulus is to blame, lead him to propose the expedition to Staffa for an uninterrupted view of the horizon. It is clear by now that Oliver and Helena are drawing ever closer and only await the sighting of the Green Ray to confirm their love. Ironically when this happens in a split second, they are too busy looking into each other's eyes and have no need to see the Green Ray to be sure of their feelings. The novel comes to a rapid conclusion as the happy couple are married in St George's church in Glasgow.

The Green Ray is quite unlike any other of Verne's novels. Although there is some resemblance between Helena and Lady Grant in *The Children of Captain Grant* and to Nell in *The*

Underground City, it is the only novel that depends on romance from beginning to end to drive the plot. Ironically, Verne declared himself to be incapable of writing love stories and, due to his perceived lack of this skill, he preferred to play down romance in his novels as he thought that romance interrupted the flow of adventure and action which were his true skill. It is true that the romantic element is somewhat understated. In discussing the character of Helena with his publisher, Verne stated that:

> The heroine should be young, but very original, excentric while still remaining proper and this must be written with a very light touch.

Certainly, Pierre-Jules Hetzel one of the most important French publishers of the nineteenth century, who often criticised Verne's manuscripts and wielded a heavy editorial pen, warmly approved of *The Green Ray*.

The book has been criticised by purist Verne scholars as being rather lightweight and even trivial. This is too harsh a judgement for although the plot may lack depth, it certainly does not lack movement. In fact the story evolves at a gentle pace, interrupted by frequent dramatic incidents, as the rescue from the Corryvreckan or the idiotic interventions of Aristobulus Ursiclus. This gentle pace allows Verne to produce some fine descriptions of the West Coast as typified by his evocation of Fingal's Cave. It is clear from correspondence and from interviews that that his 1879 journey remained with him as one of the most memorable of his travels, after all it was made almost entirely by his favourite method of travel, aboard boats. We can conclude that *The Green Ray* was a novel written with affection and personal recollection, which if not his greatest literature, was nevertheless close to his heart.

Professor Ian Thompson

Luath Press Limited
committed to publishing well written books worth reading

LUATH PRESS takes its name from Robert Burns, whose little collie Luath (*Gael.,* swift or nimble) tripped up Jean Armour at a wedding and gave him the chance to speak to the woman who was to be his wife and the abiding love of his life. Burns called one of 'The Twa Dogs' Luath after Cuchullin's hunting dog in Ossian's *Fingal*. Luath Press was established in 1981 in the heart of Burns country, and is now based a few steps up the road from Burns' first lodgings on Edinburgh's Royal Mile.

Luath offers you distinctive writing with a hint of unexpected pleasures.

Most bookshops in the UK, the US, Canada, Australia, New Zealand and parts of Europe either carry our books in stock or can order them for you. To order direct from us, please send a £sterling cheque, postal order, international money order or your credit card details (number, address of cardholder and expiry date) to us at the address below. Please add post and packing as follows: UK – £1.00 per delivery address; overseas surface mail – £2.50 per delivery address; overseas airmail – £3.50 for the first book to each delivery address, plus £1.00 for each additional book by airmail to the same address. If your order is a gift, we will happily enclose your card or message at no extra charge.

Luath Press Limited
543/2 Castlehill
The Royal Mile
Edinburgh EH1 2ND
Scotland
Telephone: 0131 225 4326 (24 hours)
Fax: 0131 225 4324
email: sales@luath.co.uk
Website: www.luath.co.uk